T0195894

Other books by Beryl Carpenter:

Discovery Series – set in 15th century Spain

Far From a Pleasant Land
Toward a Dark Horizon
When Doves Laughed

Trouble at Port Gamble

Beryl Carpenter

authorHOUSE®

AuthorHouse™
1663 Liberty Drive
Bloomington, IN 47403
www.authorhouse.com
Phone: 1 (800) 839-8640

Cover: Port Gamble Mills, Puget Mill Company Owners. From History of the Pacific Northwest: Oregon and Washington. Elwood Evans, 1892. Use courtesy of Washington State University Libraries Manuscripts, Archives, and Special Collections' Northwest Illustrations digital collection.

Back cover photo by Suzy Petrucci, Glimmer Glass Photography

Published by AuthorHouse 01/17/2020

ISBN: 978-1-7283-4075-3 (sc)
ISBN: 978-1-7283-4074-6 (e)

Library of Congress Control Number: 2019920985

Print information available on the last page.

To all who have a dream and follow it

LIST OF
CHARACTERS

Addie (Adaira) Murray Reagan – 19-year-old widow; seeking a new life as a detective

Sam Reagan – deceased husband of Addie; worker who died in a mill accident

Marcus Williams – new sawyer in Port Gamble

Simon Jamison – Pinkerton's agent based in Seattle

Cameron Murray – Addie's father; manages general store in Port Gamble

Caroline Murray – Addie's mother; unhappy; disapproves of Addie

Elliot Smith – a manager at Puget Mill Company; buys tracts of timber for the mill

*Edwin Ames – Puget Mill manager and driving force in Port Gamble (historical person)

Martha Smith – Elliott's wife; social climber; wants to marry off her daughter

Marianne Smith – sixteen-year-old daughter; a flirt and a schemer

Cochran Smith – twelve-year-old male heir; learning the company business

Jake Hardy – mill foreman; willing to take risks and cut corners on safety

Chen Liu – small Chinese boy; a servant at the Smiths' house

Chen Fu –mill worker and father of Liu; noted philosopher and educator in China

Chen Jiao – mother of Chen Liu; main cook at Mrs. Smith's

Ella Rose Flynn – cook and manager of Seaside Eatery in Port Gamble; a Quaker

Sarah Larson – postmistress at Port Gamble; best friend of Addie

Tony (Antonio) Esposito – creepy mill worker; bullies mill workers; thug for Jake Hardy

Frankie Russo—Tony's helper and thug for Jake Hardy

*Frank Hall—survivor of Custer's Last Stand, in hiding, owns a Webley Bull Dog pistol (Based on historical character Frank Finkel or Finkle)

George Frederick – Mill worker from Maine; plays on PG baseball team; likes Addie

Eddie George – S'Klallam Indian mill worker; comes over from Point Julia each day

Laura Benson – schoolteacher at Port Gamble

John and Mary Deming – pastor and wife of Union Congregational Church at Port Gamble; part-time doctor (based on historical person John Damon)

Andrew Spencer—main doctor in Port Gamble

Lydia Reed – nurse at Port Gamble hospital

Jensen, Flanagan and O'Malley—labor agitators that start a strike at the mill

ACKNOWLEDGMENTS

As always, I rely on the knowledge of others when writing. Those who have special skills or expertise are fascinating to talk to, as well.

One avid reader and interesting person is Ron Kirkland, retired career Naval officer and expert on firearms, old and new. Many thanks for helping me pick a gun for Addie to tote around, and for explaining how things work.

Thanks to Meilynn Smith for her curiosity and fine touch as a house stager. She creates environments that invite a person in. I know, because I've stayed at her cozy home. She's also Swedish and has a sense of what a Scandinavian family would say and do. Thanks for all the suggestions. I can smell the cardamom bread baking!

Thanks to best friend Janice Blair, my main nag and encourager. Her occasional postcards of Port Gamble along with a few choice words kept me moving toward completion. Another great friend, Rhoda Russell, knew when to step back and give me space when I couldn't pull it all together. Both were needed.

Bill Woodward, professor at Seattle Pacific University, listened to my ideas and made suggestions as to resources available in Kitsap County and Seattle.

As ever, Robert, my dear husband, read, edited, suggested and listened when I lamented how long it was taking. His confidence in me has been my guiding light.

Soli Deo Gloria.

CHAPTER I

"Addie—Addie!"

The voice came at her like a screeching owl. Addie peered into the growing darkness. Cold drizzle hit her face.

Light-footed steps crunched on the gravel path behind her.

"Sarah?" Suddenly, the mystery creature burst through the gloom, golden hair flying.

"Of course, it's me, silly. And I have something for you, Addie May Reagan—here." She thrust out an envelope.

"Is it the one I've been waiting for?" The words clogged Addie's throat.

"What else would it be?"

Addie tore open it open and scanned the letter. "I have an interview!"

"Hurray!" Sarah clapped her hands.

"You didn't tell anyone, did you?" Addie re-folded the letter.

"Nobody else knows."

"You're wonderful, Sarah Larson."

"I know. The best postmistress ever, right?"

Addie hugged her friend and slipped the envelope into her pocket.

"I'd better get home. My parents are expecting me." Sarah waved and ran off.

"Meet me tomorrow and I'll tell you all the details," Addie yelled after her. She hurried toward the lighted window ahead, legs churning. She raced toward her family home, holding more than a slim envelope in her pocket. It was a whole new possibility.

But, before she reached home, something caught Addie's attention—a movement of bushes, a raspy noise. What she saw made her mouth drop open as big as the winter moon rising in the sky.

A small hand pushed open a hole in the thicket of bushes just beyond the family property. Two small almond-shaped eyes appeared.

"Help me." The voice squeaked. "Could I have water, please?"

"Who are you?" Addie drew nearer. "Come out of the bushes. I'll get water."

"No stay. No tell." A little boy pushed his way through the wild roses and pulled the sticking thorns from his threadbare clothes.

Addie walked toward their back door. One dip of the tin cup tied to the pump and she handed him the cold water he wanted.

"How old are you?"

"Eight." Skinny arms covered by a homespun shirt reached out to accept the cup.

"Are you hungry? I'll get some food." Addie moved toward the door.

"No! No one know me. I run away." He turned toward the woods again.

"Wait. What's your name? Where do you live? Come back." The wind whistling around the eaves made the only reply.

"Who are you talking to out there, Addie?" Mother peeked out the door. "Come in and get out of the damp."

"Nobody, Mother. Just reciting poetry to myself. And my name's Adaira."

"Ridiculous! Dinner's waiting."

"I'll leave some food on the back porch," Addie said to the rose hedge. "Just come back and talk to me." She grabbed the handrail and swung into the steaming kitchen, closing out the dismal weather. A swirl of unanswered questions hovered outside like a swarm of mosquitos.

"Wash your hands and sit down this minute, Addie. The biscuits are on the table." Mother grabbed two greasy hot pads and swung the cast iron pot from stove to table. Addie scrubbed her hands with a splash of hot water and the strong soap Mother made. She rubbed her wet hands on the shared towel. Her chair scraped under the table just as Father's did the same. Mother frowned. Father said a quick prayer.

"How was your day, Addie, after I left the store?" Father helped himself to the stew, dipping from the top. Addie reached for a biscuit. It was cold.

"Mrs. Sloan came in and I sold her some sugar and molasses. Otherwise, it was quiet. And my name's Adaira." Addie spooned a big dollop of jam onto the biscuit and bit into it. A little jam dripped onto the tablecloth. Mother raised an eyebrow. She scooped deeply from the stew pot and plopped a spoonful in Addie's bowl.

The burned bits from the bottom again. Addie sighed. Mother couldn't cook.

"Mrs. Sloan can be troublesome," said Father. "Good stew, Mother." His spoon circled the bowl one last time. "I believe I'll have some more." He put a biscuit in his bowl and ladled stew over it. A baying hound sounded outside, then another. Addie flinched.

"Never mind, Addie," said Mother. "The guard dogs have been set loose. There must be some intruder in the town." The howl of several dogs now circled closer. In fact, it came from right outside the windows. Someone rapped on the door.

"I'll get it, Mother." Father pushed back from the table and crossed quickly to the door. "What seems to be the trouble, Jones?" He peered into the darkness.

"A runaway, Cameron. At least, we think so." The dogs' barking muffled his words. "Seen anything suspicious?"

"Can't say that I have. Well, good luck. It's a miserable night to be out."

"You're right about that. Well, better get on with it."

Father shut the door and returned to the table.

"Any dessert, Caroline—a cookie or a piece of pie, maybe? I do love your pie." He made a goofy grin. Mother's countenance cracked. A smile curved upward across her face.

"Why, Cameron, you're *such* a charmer." She hurried to the cookie jar and put a handful of cookies on a plate. Just then, a cry pierced the night.

"Caught!" yelled Father, who grabbed two sugar cookies.

Mother sighed, but Addie shuddered.

"I'll clean up the dishes and tidy the kitchen," she offered.

Mother nodded, went to pour some hot water from the copper kettle to make tea. "I believe I'll set a spell in my rocker. Goodness knows I have earned it." She carried her steaming cup into the main room.

Addie collected the bowls and cutlery, poured hot water into the dishpan and rubbed some soap onto a dishrag. The immersed dishes were soon clean. She picked up a flour sack dishtowel and rubbed them dry.

Addie thought about the boy with the almond shaped eyes. The mill hired Chinese people, as well as Indians from across the bay, but she'd never seen a child in town before. Addie put a couple of biscuits smeared red with jam onto a plate, covered it with an old cloth and stepped outside. She plopped the plate on a stump not far from the porch.

Hope this is not late.

CHAPTER 2

Addie adjusted the kerosene lamp wick in her room. Shadows scurried to the far corners like frightened spiders. Addie climbed in bed and pulled the quilt up to her chin. Damp cold filled the corner room. She reached for the book under her pillow. A Sherlock Holmes mystery, *A Study in Scarlet*, fell open to where she'd left a bookmark. She shivered and rolled over, placing the book on the pillow, her shoulders covered by the faded triangles of the blue and white quilt.

Would Mother approve? Probably not.

The whining sawmill in the distance was a constant nuisance. She stopped to listen. A few of the book's pages flipped. Addie shrugged her shoulders and tried to settle into considering the clues the odd detective found. She considered her own escape plan. She had been thinking for some time she wanted to be a detective. Mother and Father would disapprove, of course.

"What makes you think you can be a good detective?" Father would say.

"It's too dangerous for a young woman," Mother would add.

"I have skills, you know I do. I'm very observant. And I think things through. I'm strong and determined, too. I can solve puzzles. And I'm a good shot." Her rehearsed words sounded defensive and pathetic as they hung in the air.

"With a rifle, daughter." Father would make that rumbling coughing noise.

"Wait! I want to read the letter again." Addie interrupted her reverie. Addie threw aside her book and fetched the letter from her skirt pocket. Her palms dripped with sweat and her face flushed.

I have to change my life somehow. I must!

I just buried my husband in the cemetery on the hill one year ago. Three months married and already twelve month a widow. My Sam died in a mill accident here at Port Gamble. He caught a suspender in the big saw and was drawn into the razor-sharp monster. I ran to the mill when I heard. What the workers couldn't keep me from seeing was a pool of blood and one of his hands jammed in the machinery. I couldn't believe it. I still can't. Sam was my one chance at happiness.

She wiped a few tears from her eyes.

I'm not a child anymore. I need to work. And I need to find a new way. So, I'm making a plan. Before 1889 is over, I'll have a new life.

The company steamship came in regularly to unload supplies at Puget Mill operations in Port Gamble. They first began in San Francisco and then expanded to Port Gamble in 1853 to supply lumber for the California Gold Rush. *I could be on the ship when it slides out of the harbor and onto the next stop.*

I'll change my name to Adaira Reagan, a real proper name, and start a detective agency in San Francisco, where any kind of intrigue could happen. The newspapers that come on the ships say there are still lots of disputes about gold mine claims. There are bank robbers and people who try to trick the unsuspecting out of their hard-earned money. There are even complaints by Chinese immigrants who claim they were forcibly brought to America to work.

Of course, it might take a while to get started. I have a plan for that, too. It's my brightest prospect so far. I wrote to the Pinkerton Detective Agency asking to be interviewed for a job.

Addie held the reply in her hand again, gripping it tightly. If she read it again maybe it would seem more real.

It said:

> Dear Mr. Reagan,
>
> Thank you for your letter of 3 December 1888. We are always gratified when men show interest in enforcing the laws of the United States. Your credentials are adequate, though it seems you are new in your career aspirations. There is no need for you to come to San Francisco.

But, if you are determined to make good, we have a proposal for you.

Our agency has recently been asked to investigate in the very community you live: Port Gamble, Washington Territory, correct? Since it is confidential information, I cannot divulge the matter in this letter.

Contact our agency in Seattle for further information. The agent in charge there is Simon Jamison. You will need to contact him to arrange an interview.

You failed to state what kind of weapon you have. Please convey that information to Jamison. There may be an assignment for you in Port Gamble and a cash advance for expenses, should you complete the interview satisfactorily.

Best regards,
Harold Hill

Addie let out a big sigh and hugged the letter to her chest.

Now I don't have to make a fool of myself running off to San Francisco. And when I have a real job, I will have money of my own.

I could print a few business cards. I might invest in

a new jacket, too. Ann Ross is a good seamstress. I could ask her. The rest of the money I'll hide away.

Addie read the letter a third time and then folded it back into its envelope.

Why does my stomach churn and my cheeks burn? Whatever is wrong with me? After all, starting tomorrow, I'll become Adaira Reagan, investigator.

Now, there was just one problem to be solved. Or maybe two.

Addie got out of bed and knelt next to it. She clenched her hands tight.

Please help me get this job, God. I need it!

Addie grabbed the leather handles and pulled out a small trunk from underneath her bed. Snapping the locks open and lifting the lid, she looked for that small bundle wrapped in linen. She stroked Sam's dress-up shirt and brushed it against her cheek. The fine cloth slid softly through her fingers. She unwrapped the packet containing the few earthly belongings she had of Samuel Alan Reagan, her beloved husband.

Out slid a pocket watch that had been his father's. The silver case had three letters etched on the back: S. A. R., the same as Sam's initials. There was a leather cord tied onto a necklace with a key hanging on it. And, what she was looking for: Sam's gun.

He told me it was a Colt 1851 Navy revolver. Addie hefted it and felt the smooth curve of the handle in her hand—not too heavy, with smooth wood and a patriotic scenic engraved on the metal sides. It was almost an antique in 1889.

I don't know a lot about guns, but I know it has been converted to take .44 caliber bullets. Sam favored it for its quick firing action. Sam showed it to me before he died. The recoil made me tumble backwards into Sam's arms. After sharing a good laugh, Sam said, "If anything happens to me, use my gun for protection."

I'll tell Mr. Jamison I have a Colt 1851 Navy revolver with modifications. That will put me in favor. After all, I know the Pinkerton brothers use the same model. Hopefully, I won't need it for a long time.

Addie re-wrapped the gun in the linen shirt and stowed it away. The trunk scraped across the floor as she pushed it back.

Addie sat up on the bed and brushed her caramel-colored hair, the color of coffee with thick cream mixed in, Sam always said. After she braided it for sleeping, she washed her face and hands in the china basin, the soap a thin sliver. Addie wiped her teeth with a bit of Colgate dentifrice and then swished some water around in her mouth. She spat into the basin of used water.

Was all this fuss with teeth really worth it?

Addie picked her way back across the floor as if barefoot on a sheet of ice. She grabbed some wooly socks and slipped them on. Leaning over to reach the lamp, Addie turned down the wick till the light went out and swung her legs under the cold sheets.

Traceries of rain streaked down the window.

I can't stop thinking about the little boy. Who is he? Where is his mother? And father? Are they servants of someone here in Port Gamble? I'll have to find out.

Then, there was the possible new assignment from Pinkerton.

I could start my agency—or at least get a job.

Addie smiled and sank into her pillow.

Now I only have to convince Pinkerton's to hire me.

CHAPTER 3

"Tell me what the letter said. I'm dying to know." Sarah sat down next to Addie at the corner table in Seaside Place, our usual meeting spot.

"First, let's order something."

Ella Rose padded over to their table, her footfalls rattling the daisy-flowered sugar pot. "What will it be, girls? Speak!"

"Do you have any good coffee, Ella?" Addie asked.

"Yep, freshly roasted beans from South America. The last ship unloaded them three days ago." Ella Rose shifted her canoe-sized shoes on the bare boards, gritty with a thin layer of sand and sawdust.

"Then, two coffees and two pieces of your wonderful ginger cake."

"Oh, so you're celebrating," said Ella Rose. She twisted a loose strand of salt and pepper hair into her bun.

"Maybe," Addie said, and smiled. Ella Rose wrote down the order.

"Come up to the counter to pick up your order when I call you. I've got walnut loaves in the oven to watch." She stumped back to the counter to cut the cake.

"Don't tell anyone. Please, Sarah." Addie straightened her posture to look at her friend directly. "I'm to report to the Seattle office of Pinkerton's for an interview with Simon Jamison." Addie raised her eyebrows and felt a smile spread across her face.

"Sounds promising. Be sure to ask him a lot of questions," said Sarah. "Like working conditions and salary." She squeezed Addie's arm.

"Coffee here is usually that awful chicory," Addie said to steer the conversation in a less personal direction. "Smells like burned rags and tastes like them, too."

Sarah giggled and nodded her head, then looked directly at Addie.

"That's wonderful that you have an interview! When will you go?"

"As soon as I can arrange it," Addie said. "I'll send a letter on the next boat, asking for an appointment."

"Why did they offer you a job? I mean—we both know you have no experience." Sarah bit her lip and looked down.

"That's mean," Addie said, the words still stinging. "But true."

"Order!" Ella Rose called. Sarah hopped up and fetched the tray containing the coffee and cakes.

"Sorry, but we did talk about it, didn't we?"

Sarah placed a china cup of pungent coffee and a white plate of golden dense-grained cake dusted with powdered sugar in front of Addie and then reached for a piece. She grabbed a cup and sipped the coffee.

"Mm, heavenly!"

Addie nodded and took a forkful of ginger cake. "I really need to prepare for the interview. I could use your help. It won't be easy to convince them. After all, I'm a woman, young and with no special training." Addie sighed and traced a design on her plate with her fork.

"Tell them about your special gift of noticing things," said Sarah. "Remember when you found Mrs. Smith's missing pearl necklace?"

"Oh, that. She got hysterical that one of her servants took them. She even offered a reward." Addie covered her mouth, but a snicker burst out.

"And, what did you discover?" Sarah coaxed the story out of her.

"Well, you know. I went to her and asked if I could look around her house. I was there to practice a duet with her daughter, Marianne, for the talent show. I asked her some questions about when she last wore them and so on. I checked between the cushions of the parlor sofa, asked again and then suggested she look under her bed.

"Have you had any problems with your servants before?" I asked. "Mrs. Smith shrugged her shoulders and sighed. Her hair was uncombed, and her eyes were red. I suggested she look in her room. While she went upstairs, Marianne and I sat down to start working on our piece. The piano had a key that plunked. It was hard to get through the music. I told Marianne to stop. I looked inside the piano where all the strings are."

"And there it was! Right?"

"Well, I found one pearl. Mrs. Smith came back at that precise moment. I told her I guessed she had argued with Mr. Smith the night before. She burst into tears. I made her sit down and compose herself, calling for a tea tray even."

"Clever of you," said Sarah. "Did you find out why she accused the servants?"

"I knew Mrs. Smith was deflecting the guilt she felt. Mrs. Smith ripped off the necklace in the heat of the argument and the beads flew everywhere, she said. She opened her hand and there was a pile of shiny pearls in her palm. She said she gathered them up after Mr. Smith left the room. Mrs. Smith drank the chamomile tea I ordered and then decided to go lie down. I gave her the one pearl I found and told her I'd give her apologies to the servants if she would reconcile with Mr. Smith that evening. She nodded while looking at the pile of beads she held."

"Such unbecoming behavior," said Sarah. "Did it all work out?"

"Mrs. Smith was embarrassed, I think, but promised to speak to Mr. Smith. She's been more cordial to me since then, but, really, I just had a hunch. Marianne told me before that her mother was subject to fits of rage."

"Tell Mr. Jamison about those hunches," said Sarah. "I mean it. Think of some other times you've done that. You really have a gift."

"Thanks, but I still have another problem. I'm a woman."

"Pinkerton had a famous female detective that solved the murder of President Lincoln. You told me that."

"That's true. They also will want to know if I can shoot a pistol."

"Can you? Do you even have a gun?"

"Sam left me one."

"And—?"

"He taught me how to shoot. But it kicks as strong as a wild horse."

"As if you didn't know that would happen. Well, you can work on that."

"Yes, or I can get a derringer, a woman's gun."

"That will take a while. You'll have to save some money." Sarah pushed her empty plate away and reached for her purse. "I really should go."

"I'm paying." Addie put out her hand to stop Sarah from pulling out some coins. "I have some money from my job at the general store."

"Truly? Well, thank you." Sarah stood up and gave her a little hug.

"Wait! What should I wear?" Adaira grabbed Saran's arm.

"My Sunday dress is too *frou-frou*—you know— fancy and embellished. I have a black woolen dress, fitted at the waist, with a small ruffle at the neck. Would that do?"

"Yes, wear the black dress and hold your head up high. You'll do very well," said Sarah. She hurried out.

"Goodbye and thanks," said Addie to her friend's retreating figure. "I hope you're right." She sighed and set down money on the little table. Taking her friend's advice, she straightened her posture and practiced gliding out of the little café with confidence. As she moved through the cluster of tables, she caught a foot in the leg of a chair, lurched forward and put out her hand just in time to prevent a fall. A young man seated at the adjacent table reached out to steady her. His deep blue eyes fastened onto hers.

"Are you all right?" he said, and stood up.

"Fine," Addie mumbled and brushed by him, her face crimson. She headed for the door like a rat escaping a sinking ship.

"Well, Adaira Reagan," she muttered under her breath, "Clearly you need to do some work before you have that interview."

CHAPTER 4

Marcus Williams pushed his empty plate away from him and brought the linen napkin to his lips. He brushed crumbs off his neat red mustache.

"Thank you ever so much, Mrs. Smith. That was a tasty dinner."

"You're welcome, Mr. Williams. A hard-working young man like you needs plenty of food. I hope you got enough." She pushed a plate of rolls toward him.

"No, no. I couldn't eat another bite. I'm bursting." He patted his trim middle. "I sure appreciate you renting me a room. I hear the dormitories are undesirable."

"They're filthy—vermin infested and all." Mrs. Smith shuddered.

"And the smell is unbearable," said Marianne. She sniffed and wiggled her nose.

"Stinky," added Cochran, and plugged his nose.

"Hush. How would you two know that?" Mrs. Smith narrowed her eyes and set her mouth in a thin line. Marianne lowered her eyes, but Cochran stifled a laugh.

"Think nothing of it, Williams," continued Mr. Smith. "You're the new sawyer for Puget Mill Company. We need to treat you with respect." Mr. Smith put a hand in his vest pocket and drew out a watch.

"I do plan to build a house as soon as I save enough money," said Marcus.

"That shouldn't be too long with your fine wages." Mr. Smith stroked his mustache.

"Yes, I'm grateful. I'm hoping to make a new start here."

"A lot of men come to Port Gamble for that reason. Hope you make a go of it." Mr. Smith clapped Marcus on the shoulder as he got up from the table.

"A fine dinner, Martha," he said, giving his wife a smile with eyes that crinkled at the edges.

"Thank you, Elliot." Mrs. Smith colored. Cochran waited for a nod from his mother, then jumped up and followed his father.

"Marianne, go and practice." The girl padded away with a sigh and rustle of skirts.

"I'll excuse myself, too." Marcus pushed his chair back and laid the napkin next to his plate. He exited the room, the swirling vines of the wallpaper making him dizzy. He heard piano music starting. He climbed the stairs to his second-floor room.

The Smith family lived in a large house on executive row. The mansion had eight bedrooms and two bathrooms, a large parlor and dining room, a conservatory, an office for Mr. Smith, and servants' quarters on the third floor. Some of the servants were Chinese, Mrs. Smith said, but she kept them in the kitchen, so they were never seen.

Mr. Elliot Smith was an agent of Puget Mill Company. He spent a sizable part of his days buying up acres of virgin forest. He kept quiet about it, but sometimes he had visitors come into his mahogany-paneled office in the evening and the conversations droned on a long time. He was there now, no doubt, teaching his son the trade. Cochran was twelve and Marianne sixteen. Three other daughters had grown up and married.

Marcus entered his room and closed the door. The top panel had a frosted windowpane that could be opened for air circulation. The single bed had a polished brass frame and several wool blankets. All the bedrooms had small fireplaces, but his had no wood in it. Mrs. Smith said he must pay for that and he hadn't received his first month's pay yet. The room did have a modern sink with a mirror above, though. And a kerosene lamp that sent golden light to all the dark corners as he turned up the wick. It sat on a small table. With a chair, narrow dresser and rag rug, the room was almost welcoming.

Marcus removed his shoes and lowered his body onto the bed. He drew a book toward him, *The Adventures of Huckleberry Finn*.

Would my mother approve? Probably not, but I find

the wild abandon of the hero fascinating. I'll read just a few more pages.

5:20 in the morning came early. That's when the first horn blew, warning workers to get up. Mrs. Smith would set out hot oatmeal, milk and strong coffee on the buffet. To be more precise, she would have the servants put it out. When the next horn bellows twenty minutes later, it was off to work. All must be on the job by six in the morning.

Marcus dropped the book after two pages and reviewed the first week's work. Sharpening saws was an exacting occupation. His father had taught him all he knew and then had apprenticed him to Henry Evans, the finest sawyer in East Machias, Maine. It was a much-needed trade and brought a good wage. The circular and band saws needed to be razor-sharp to rip through the old-growth giants from these northwest forests.

I had to leave Maine in a hurry. Hope nobody finds out the reason.

Marcus yawned. He put the book on the table, setting his Bible on top. Ten minutes later he slipped under the crisp sheets. The rain was driving against the window.

That interesting girl in the café today-- awkward but determined. I'll have to find out her name. Marcus folded the pillow under his head and settled in.

Please, God, let me make good here. I need the money.

CHAPTER 5

The kitchen door pushed open and Martha Smith marched in.

"Mrs. Chen, I must speak to you."

Mrs. Chen put down a cleaver and sharpening stone and came to stand in front of Mrs. Smith. Mrs. Chen bowed several times. If she had questions, her face didn't show it.

Mrs. Smith proceeded.

"Your child, Liu, ran away today. He has just been caught and returned to me. You'll find him in the basement."

"Yes, madam." Mrs. Chen bobbed her head several times.

"Finish up your work here and take him back to your quarters. See to it he doesn't do that again, or he'll be severely punished." Mrs. Smith swished out of the kitchen.

Chen Jiao's knuckles turned white and her face red as she returned to her duties. She took up the cleaver and drove the blade deep into the chopping block. The blade sank in and stuck. Mrs. Chen let go and left it there a moment. She spoke a few words to the dishwasher, Flora, who poured a final rinse of hot water from the kettle into the sink, swished her dishrag around. She wrung it clean. The dishes dried in the cool air. Flora put them back in their proper places and untied her apron. She grabbed up her coat and hat and slipped out the door.

Jiao pulled the cleaver out of the wooden block and slid it into its place in the drawer, sighing. She trudged down the narrow stairs to the basement and opened a small door. Liu looked up and ran to his mother. She enveloped him in her arms, squatting down to better hold him.

"Liu, why you run away?" She smoothed his black hair back from a sweaty forehead. In spite of the hot stove for heating the irons, Mrs. Chen shivered.

"Cold and dark here. Only a small window there." Liu pointed to a dark pane behind him. "I wanted to be outside, to see the trees blow and see the big bird that flies."

"Be careful. Get work done first, Liu."

"Dark when I get up. Dark when go home. When can I see bird that flies, Mother?" Liu looked down at his feet.

"I find way to get you out every day." Mrs. Chen set her jaw and lifted her chin. "Boy should see bird that flies. Called 'eagle.' Now, come. We go home." She helped him stoke the fire and close the little window. They held hands and climbed the stairs and went out the back way, closing the door on another long day. It was cold outside. The misty air settled onto their shoulders.

"Hurry, we must get dining room. All food is fast eaten." They trotted down the path leading to the hall for Chinese workers, about two blocks away. They burst into a hot room full of Chinese sounds. Chairs scraped as they were pulled up to the long table that filled the center of the room.

"I'm here, Jiao." Mr. Chen stood up and ushered them to the spots he'd saved for them. Just then, steaming bowls of food came out of the kitchen. Jiao plugged her nose.

"Let's pretend it's the finest Chinese food. What do you see, Liu?"

"I want Shanghai dumplings and steamed *bok choy* with garlic." He licked his lips.

"I'll have fermented bean curd with green flower vegetable," said Mr. Chen, his English the best in their family.

"Only me hot and sour soup." Mrs. Chen peered into the bowl of sticky brown beans being passed. She took a spoonful and then a spoonful of thick mush from the next bowl. "At least, we get some meat every Sunday."

They all sighed for an instant.

"Eat fast now, it's the only way to get your share." Mr. Chen took a large spoonful and chewed vigorously. All the Chinese words in the room clattered to the floor and disappeared as the people at the table filled their stomachs. Then, they all got up and brought dirty dishes to the kitchen workers, who had eaten by themselves. They all helped clean the kitchen and sweep the floor. Tired by their long day of work, they all filed out silently and made their way to their small family rooms down the hall. It was seven-thirty.

"Tomorrow starts early," said Mrs. Chen. They nodded. Liu yawned and peeled off his work clothes. He put on the nightshirt and scratched his arms. Mrs. Chen kneeled by his bed and whispered a few words to him.

"I'm proud of you, Liu. You are a clever boy. Don't get discouraged. We will find a way." She gave him a peck on his cheek and patted his shoulder through the thin quilts.

She turned and walked a few paces to the double bed that filled the rest of the room. Chen Fu, her husband, lay on his side, opening the covers for her. She donned her long nightgown with the Mandarin collar and joined him. They held each other for a long time and whispered the events of their days to each other.

"How will we survive here, Fu?" Jiao snuggled closer to her husband.

"We will find a way. And remember, there will be less work tomorrow.

CHAPTER 6

Sunday dawned gray and dreary. A biting wind blew in from the Juan de Fuca strait. Addie helped her mother slice the crusty bread for breakfast. She slipped it under the broiler in the big country stove. She measured coffee spoon by spoon into the kettle. The aroma took over the room, dominant as the creosote pilings on the dock. She thought about the oily stickiness that coated the piers and made rainbow rings in the salt water. Then she smelled something burning.

"Oh, the toast!" and grabbed the cooking tray with the help of a potholder. The bread's edges were black, but the rest could be rescued. She scraped the charred parts and then dabbed them with butter. After piling the bread on a plate, she got out the jar of blackberry preserves. Mother walked in and grabbed the stack of bread, sniffing the air.

"We must hurry breakfast, or we'll be late for church," she said.

"I'll bring the jam and coffee," said Addie, and followed Mother into the small dining room.

"It was mighty hard to wake up this morning,"

said Father, placing a napkin in his lap. "So cold and windy." He reached for two slices of toast.

"Now, Cameron, first we'll ask the blessing." Mother bowed her head and began thanking God for the food and ending minutes later after asking a blessing on Aunt Matilda, Uncle Henry, the pastor's sermon and the President of the United States. Addie sighed but kept her eyes closed. They ate the toast and coffee without speaking. Addie cleared the table and set the dishes to soak. Mother and Father were waiting at the door when she came down the stairs with her bonnet and Bible.

"It's only two blocks to the church," said Mother, "but I fear we're a few minutes late." She made a disapproving sound in her throat.

"Nonsense, we can find a back pew to sit in," said Father, starting out the door. He threw a mackintosh over his Sunday suit. Mother opened her umbrella and scurried after him. Addie grabbed the glass doorknob of the front door and closed it behind them. She put a shawl over her shoulders. The Murrays made their way across the graveled road and along a board sidewalk toward the towering steeple. They pushed into the entry, shook out their umbrellas and found the back row held a couple of Chinese workers. Mother scowled and moved forward a row.

Addie slipped in after her mother and father. She took the damp shawl off her shoulders and folded it across the arm of the pew. Reverend

Deming led the congregation in singing "Blessed Assurance," a favorite of Addie's. She joined in with her uncertain soprano, trying her best to blend in with the other voices around her. She glanced to each side and saw ocean blue eyes looking her way. She turned her glance back to the front.

After the singing, the pastor spoke from the book of James about the need to ask for God's direction in living your life.

"When you ask for wisdom, believe that you will receive it. Move ahead in faith that God will guide you," he said. "Look for his direction and his provision. He'll never fail you." Pastor Deming dismissed the congregation with a blessing and filed down the aisle to take his place at the entry. People crowded toward the pastor and each person wanted to shake his hand, it seemed. Addie was one of the first, slipping out of the next to back pew. The soggy shawl felt like a wet dog on her arm.

"Thank you, Pastor Deming. I'm Addie Reagan, remember? I really like it when you preach on an encouraging subject." She shook his warm hand and then sidled out the doorway. She nodded to Mrs. Deming, and then strode out to stand in a spot of sunshine breaking through the gray sky. She took a deep breath of the rain-washed smell of fir, spruce and hemlock.

"There's nothing finer than a day with unexpected sunshine," said a deep voice behind her.

"I agree with all my heart," said Addie as she

whirled around. She caught her breath. There stood the young man with eyes as blue as a bottomless lake. He took off his hat and fingered it with both hands. His sandy hair glowed in the sunlight. "I've seen you before, haven't I?" she said.

"I believe we met in Seaside Place yesterday," he said. "You nearly fell at my feet." Smooth lips curved upward. "My name is Marcus Williams," he said.

"I'm Addie Reagan." Her cheeks colored as she offered her hand. He held it for a moment in his own firm one. Just then the shawl slipped off her arm and landed on his boot.

"Oh, not again!" she said. Addie reached down to pick it up. Their heads collided as he did the same thing. She covered her eyes. He chuckled.

"That's me," said Addie. "I'm clumsy. You might as well know it now." She started to walk away.

"Wait, I don't mind. My brother has a crippling palsy. I often help him as he walks. Now he needs one of those new wheeled chairs."

"Oh, so you think I'm crippled?" She turned away again.

"I didn't mean that!" Marcus laid a light hand on her arm. "I just meant your momentary problems are nothing. I don't mind them at all."

"But I do have a problem, is that it?" Addie's elevating voice was attracting attention.

Marcus pursed his lips and sighed. "Please

forgive me. I'm making a mess of this. Yesterday, I saw something in your eyes. It looked like determination. I just wanted to meet you." He looked down at his shoes. "Could we start again?"

Addie took a deep breath and felt the tightness in her body subside. "I forgive you. It's really my fault. Whenever I get tense, I have little accidents. That usually ends the acquaintance." She smiled a lips-together grin and looked at him. "You make me nervous for some reason."

"I'm the new sawyer in town. I've been here about a week," said Marcus.

"It's nice to meet you," said Addie. "Do you like it here?"

"It's really cold and dreary. What do you do to raise your spirits?"

"We have lots of social events here. The mill owners organize them."

"Will you be attending the next social?

"The one on Friday?" said Addie. "I think so."

"It's a talent show, I heard. Are you performing?" Marcus adjusted his shirt cuffs and shifted his feet.

"I might. I haven't quite decided." Addie smoothed her hair back. She looked around. Her mother was waving toward her. "Oh, I've got to go," she said. "My mother gets jittery if dinner is late. The roast might burn." She shrugged.

"Will I see you there? Could we sit together?" He leaned forward on his toes.

"Yes. Yes, I'd enjoy that. See you then." Addie

brushed by him, trailing a faint odor of lavender and burnt toast. Marcus smiled. He plopped his hat on his sandy locks and headed toward the Smiths' house and dinner.

"Hey, lady!" Addie heard a little voice as she walked across the lawn the opposite direction. She looked around. The small Chinese boy peeked around a large maple tree, bare branches scratching at the sky.

"Yes?"

"We talk tonight? I be your house." He ran away.

CHAPTER 7

Addie sat at the dinner table and listened to the conversation. They all ate yesterday's cold sliced chicken. Mother always soaked a quart of beans on Saturday and then put it in the back compartment of the oven to cook overnight. She dosed it liberally with thick molasses and some ham or sausage scraps. The smell of it cooking had filled Addie's dreams by dawn. Long before the time Sunday dinner came, the wonderful concoction caused her stomach to gurgle with delight.

Addie took a big helping of the beans and a few slices of cold chicken. Mother brought out a cabbage slaw and day-old rolls with creamy butter and preserves. Then Mother set out custard kept cold in the root cellar. All the heavy food made the mandatory afternoon's inactivity hard to manage. Her parents insisted on resting on the Sabbath. That meant no work, no reading, unless it was the Bible, and no straying from the straight-backed chairs they sat in. Addie ended up nodding off most Sundays, only to be awakened by her mother.

This day, though, Addie thought about the

twists and turns of her recent life, especially that heart-wrenching day almost a year ago.

That day was seared in her mind. It happened as it usually did. Each time the door opened in the general store, salt air from the tidal flats rushed in. It almost made her retch. Now, just the thought of that smell brought back the events to her mind. Her insides were churning waves. Her mind raced off on a tangent. Which odor was more pungent: the pickle barrel in the back of the store or the outdoors? She gazed out the window at the dense forest around the tiny settlement she called home. Port Gamble—

She remembered the door jingling.

"Hello, Mrs. Sloan. A good afternoon to you." Addie straightened her shoulder blades.

"I need five pounds of flour and a two pounds of sugar, Addie. And if the price is right, I'll buy some calico." She sidled over to the bolts of fabric and fingered a gray and madder red pattern.

"Please call me Adaira Reagan. I was married, you know." Mrs. Sloan narrowed her eyes, but she didn't reply for a moment.

"Very well—Adaira."

"The price listed is what we charge to your account. The rates are set by the Puget Mill Company, you remember."

"Yes, I know, but I don't like it. They could charge us any amount and we'd have to pay it."

She lowered her voice and whispered, "I suspect they're robbing us, little by little."

A pain sharp as a knitting needle stabbed Addie's abdomen. She winced.

"Do you like that fabric, Mrs. Sloan? I'd be glad to cut whatever you need." Addie walked over and reached for the bolt. Unwinding it a bit, she draped the colorful swirling flowers across the counter. Mrs. Sloan fixed her eyes on it for half a minute.

"A bit loud, but my daughter likes bright colors." She folded her hands across her ample abdomen. "I'll indulge her. I'll take five yards."

"If you'd like to look around, I'll have your things ready in a jiffy." Addie smiled and got to work, even though she wanted to clutch her middle. Mrs. Sloan sniffed and went to inspect the display of preserves. Addie stretched the fabric between the lines marked on the counter and measured out five yards. She cut it with the scissors she retrieved from under the counter.

Again, the pain stabbed her insides. All of a sudden, Addie's body convulsed sending a wash of water and bloody tissue down between her legs and onto the floor. She collapsed in a heap. She guessed her face must be whiter than beach sand. Then her face warmed as she surveyed the disordered mess her body had deposited for all to see. She looked for a towel or a scarf to cover it, this thing on the floor, but she could only groan and hold her middle. It couldn't have happened in a worse place—her father's store. And Mrs. Sloan was there to see it all. Addie closed her eyes and moaned softly.

Moving quickly, Mrs. Sloan came to Addie and held her hand. She ordered Father to get a towel and some hot water and sent another shopper to get her mother.

"You've had a miscarriage, Addie, dear. I had one myself and was mortified by all the blood. Lie very still and someone will get the doctor. I'm so sorry for your pain now and for what you will experience in the next days." She took Addie's hand and patted it. Mrs. Sloan didn't leave her until the doctor arrived.

Addie shuddered. So, besides losing her husband, Addie had lost Sam's child, the last remnant of her hoped-for life that wouldn't be. After recalling that horrible event, Addie slumped in the rigid chair. She squeezed her eyes shut to will the painful thoughts away from her mind.

Addie returned to her Sunday reverie.

She had spent two days in the hospital. Nurse Reed put her in a bed with curtains around it and gave her some laudanum for the pain, and a cup of lady's mantle and sage tea to slow the bleeding.

"Let me sleep, Lydia. I need to sleep, and I don't want visitors. There's nothing I can say. And I don't want people trying to cheer me up."

"Your mother and father are here, you know. They're concerned."

"Not even them. I can't face anyone right now. Help them understand."

Nurse Lydia Reed frowned. "Is that good for you, Addie? You need comforting and kindness."

"I just can't," said Addie and turned to face the wall. Her sobs came then and shook her body. After she had cried for an hour, Lydia brought in her parents.

"I'm so sorry, Addie," said her father. "Rest and get well in body." He embraced her and planted a kiss on her tear-streaked cheek.

"I didn't know you were with child, Addie," said Mother. "What a great tragedy for you—for us all." She wiped tears from Addie's face and plumped her pillow. "We can care for you at home, you know." Addie shook her head and closed her eyes.

"Come home, Caroline. Addie's overcome. Let her be." Mr. Murray took his wife's arm and steered her out of the hospital cubicle.

I feel empty, lost. Yes, I'm feeling a bit stronger than yesterday. But, how does a person get over all the pain, all the loss? So far, I don't know how to get out of the dark woods I'm traveling through. If only I could find a way.

Someone tell me how.

As she lay there with eyes closed, Addie felt a presence sweep into the room. A rustling of skirts, a clearing of the throat, and then words she'd never forget.

"God is near the brokenhearted, Addie. Rest in his care."

As the tears streaked down Addie's face, that calm presence remained. Addie sank deeper into the bed and drifted into sleep. She didn't know when that person left, but when she opened her eyes to the new day, a faint fragrance of lavender lingered in the air.

CHAPTER 8

Pastor Deming had a problem and he couldn't keep it secret much longer. He recalled when he first came to Union Congregational Church in Port Gamble. That was several years ago now. The deacon board made it very clear what they expected.

"You must never be soft when it comes to sin. Preach against the devil. Tell of his devious ways and how we mortals must avoid his snares. Your sermons must frighten the evil out of everyone's heart. Even the children must hear of the many sins they can fall into. Do you understand?"

John Deming looked at the stern set of each deacon's face. Deacon Flynn pushed his glasses up his nose and sniffed. Deacon Erickson checked his pocket watch. But Deacon Smith frowned and folded his fingers over his ample middle. Deming began to sweat.

"Do you understand, Parson?"

"Yes, sirs. I've tried to carry that out over the years. I heartily agree and will do my utmost to convey the peril of hell to all members of the congregation." He pulled at his collar. "Of course, sometimes I feel God telling me to preach about his love." The preacher looked from face to face for support.

"Absolutely not. Let me say it again," said Deacon Smith. "Preach for our souls' good, not our comfort. We'll be listening to each sermon with that in mind. It will most certainly affect your salary, I can tell you," said Deacon Smith, jabbing an index finger in Pastor Deming's direction.

"We'll not warn you again," added Deacon Flynn. Pastor Deming murmured words of agreement and the meeting was adjourned.

Deming strolled down the sidewalk toward Seaside Place and found a seat at the counter. "I'll have coffee—strong and black," he said to the woman who stepped in front of him. He drummed his fingers on the scrubbed wooden surface. Then, he pulled a handkerchief out of his pocket and wiped it across his nose, pausing to take a big whiff. As he stuffed it in his side pocket again, an unguarded look flashed over his face—and the waitress noticed.

"Are you all right, Parson?"

"What's your name, madam?" he asked.

"Ella Rose."

Pastor Deming nodded and took a big gulp of coffee as soon as the cup was set in front of him. "Ah!" He smiled and took a few more sips. He slumped down a bit and crossed his legs. The lines on his face smoothed out. After a while, he spoke with a loud voice.

"I'll have another, please, Ella Rose," and held up the pottery mug. He sipped the rich brew and chuckled. He rolled his eyes and shut them a minute, then shook his head.

"I need to get home and tell Mary about the deacon's meeting," he said to himself. He put a few coins on the counter and slid himself off the narrow stool. "I'll have to indulge myself again. I feel extraordinary."

Deming got up and shoved his chair back.

I'll switch to nighttime starting this evening, after Mary falls asleep. That way I won't bother her. Nobody will notice.

Pastor Deming plodded home, the eternal drizzle spraying his face and dripping off his nose. He mounted the porch and entered into a very different climate.

"Mary, it's like a paradise here," he said to his wife, planting a kiss on her soft lips. "So warm and scented with spices."

"Now, John, you know I was planning to bake today." She lifted a pan from the oven. "It's gingerbread."

"Do you have any whipped cream, Mary?"

"Your favorite topping, right? Why, yes I do." She wiped her moist brow and lifted her delphinium blue eyes up to her husband. "Anything for you, dear."

John Deming smiled and held her gaze a long time.

"I don't deserve you," he said. "You're an angel." He embraced her and placed a firm kiss on her pink lips.

Mary's smile melted him like butter on hot toast. "Dinner will be ready shortly, dear. The children are waiting for you in the parlor." Deming washed his hands in the utility sink by the back door. He went in to kiss his daughter and poke his son.

Soon, Mary called them to a dinner of roast chicken, creamy mashed potatoes and carrot salad. After dinner, the parson made his way through a game of checkers with Johnny and a little tea party with Lizzie and her doll.

After she put the children to bed, John Deming embraced his wife. "You're a dear wife in every way. Thank you for the lovely evening." He kissed her willing lips.

"You sound like you're leaving, John." She leaned into his chest.

"No, but I have some studying to do on my sermon. I hope you won't mind if I stay up late in my study and do some research in the commentaries. You won't mind, will you, Mary?" John looked at her and gave her his best smile.

"Shall I wait up for you?" Her eyes roved his face for an answer.

"No need, my sweet. It's hard to say how long

I'll be." His smile receded to a straight line. He released his embrace and turned her around. He gave her a little nudge. "Now, you go along to bed. I'll be there in a while."

"Very well, John. Don't stay up too late. You need your rest." Mary swished away with soft steps. He watched her sky-blue skirts sway as she walked down the hall. When he heard the door click behind her, he stepped into his office and study. It was solely dedicated to his books and Bibles. Those books included a few medical tomes, too, for he doubled as part-time physician at Port Gamble.

He sat down heavily in his swivel chair and leaned back. He patted his coat pocket. It was too easy for him. He had picked up a small bottle of the stuff today while sewing up a few cuts and applying clean bandages to the usual number of injured mill workers.

Once, he'd sedated a man who had sliced a fingertip off. After a great fight to stop the bleeding, he applied the blessed liquid to a mesh bandage placed over the man's nose. Nurse Reed had assisted, calming the patient until he fell asleep.

Chloroform's odor was elusive—one whiff and you felt happy, like you could float on a cloud and the next whiff you moved into a deep tranquil state. On that occasion, it was all he could do to keep from sniffing the enticing, sweet smell. He had a job to do and stitched the skin back together over the remaining finger joints as quickly as he could. It was not good, the books said, to keep a patient under for too long. When the patient woke up, Deming gave him a small bottle of laudanum and sent him home.

Recently, he'd tried two drops on occasion, but when Ella Rose started noticing his behavior, the parson realized he must not let it get in the way of his daily duties. So, tonight, he'd change strategies. He would take just one sniff tonight while examining his books and planning his next scorching sermon. One whiff and he could accomplish anything. One drop and he thought of words he'd never put together before. Images flashed into his mind and out with alarming quickness. He felt bold, brave-- unstoppable. He took out the bottle and dashed a drop into his handkerchief.

Better take out a few books first. He turned around and pulled out a commentary and slapped it down on the desk.

Now I'm ready. He brought the handkerchief to his nose.

Come, Friend.

Gradually, Pastor Deming made it a habit to step in twice a day to Seaside Place and really could have come a third time. He chatted with all the people of the town. So many came to the bakery to sample Ella Rose's bakery goods. He didn't have a pastry every time he stopped by. It was really the handkerchief that enticed him. That drop of chloroform on it lasted much of the day in his pocket and he could pretend to tend a running nose almost any time. That pleasant feeling he got in the beginning helped him deliver on Sunday those pulpit-pounding sermons on "the sin that so easily besets us."

He looked down at his empty coffee cup and thought about ordering another. While waiting for each refill he yearned to swipe the infused handkerchief across his nose. The habit had increased slowly but steadily and would soon become a problem. Maybe.

"Coffee three times a day. That's quite a habit you got," said Ella Rose, the main waitress and baker. "Or maybe it's the ginger cake." Her eyes twinkled. She was right, but that was not the half of it. It sometimes scared him to think how much he depended on the chloroform to bolster his courage in the pulpit. He was becoming entirely too attached to the stuff. Not that he was addicted, like some people were claiming happened after a while. He must find a way to stop, but still keep his courage to singe his church members with the fires of hell.

"Too many weddings, Ella Rose," said the pastor. "I've conducted six weddings in the past ten days. "Soon I'll be known as the Marrying Preacher. I've stopped by here for a little refreshment after each one. And, yes, your sweet rolls are a temptation." Pastor Deming smiled at her and went back to his coffee.

Have I developed any telling mannerisms? Sweating, sallow face, trembling hands? He extended them over the table. They were soft with clean cuticles and nails trimmed straight across, but they didn't shake.

No, thank God. But I'm walking a tightrope. One misstep and all is lost. Nobody must find out. Ever.

If only I could preach a sermon on Jesus' love. That's where my heart is. But the deacons say no. What will I do this Sunday?

CHAPTER 9

Simon Jamison adjusted his tie and patted his slicked back fair hair. He held his hat on his head, because the wind kept stealing it away. Jamison shivered as he stepped from the dock onto the passenger steamboat *Nora*. It scraped against the pier and rocked with a thud. He staggered like a drunkard until he got his balance again. Soon the crew cast off from Colman Pier in Elliott Bay. Seagulls screeched word-like squawks only they understood. They circled overhead riding the wind gusts. Standing at the rail, Jamison surveyed the wintry scene.

The bay cut deep into Washington Territory. Elliott Bay presented a sheltered harbor and a long curve of shoreline to those seeking anchorage. Waves lapped at the sides of the boat. As the wind shifted, the briny stink of dockside sea life made Jamison wrinkle his nose. Here on the east side of the estuary Seattle clung to the shoreline like a colony of oysters to a rock. Or sharp barnacles perhaps--he spotted them as he looked through the clear water to the crusted pilings.

"Welcome aboard," shouted the first mate.

"Today we'll make stops at Kingston, Port Gamble, Seabeck, Brinnon, Holly, Dewatto, Lilliwaup Falls, Hoodsport and finally Union City. There are fifty souls on board plus the crew. You'll find seating inside."

The first mate finished his duties and climbed a ladder to the captain's deck. Steam engines filled the air with clanking and whirring as the boat pushed off and turned northwest toward the first destination. Jamison took a deep gulp of air and then went inside the window-lined boat. The *Nora* was on its way.

When Jamison first got the letter from the San Francisco office to go to Port Gamble, he welcomed the opportunity. He'd relocated to Seattle a year earlier. He remembered the experience, sighed and he sat down on the shellacked wooden bench.

When I first arrived here, I didn't know what to expect. But now I know the climate is much like San Francisco's. I was used to the damp drizzle and gray skies. Now, on the occasional clear day, I enjoy the spectacular views. And it's always green.

"Is this your first time sailing to the Kitsap Peninsula?" asked a lady with an enormous hat. As she leaned toward him, Jamison had to duck his head to avoid getting clipped by the lady's hat brim.

"I've never set foot outside the big city, madam," he said, removing his bowler hat to his lap. "I'm new to the Seattle area, and curious to see the outlying forests of the Washington Territory." He smiled. Seattle was not yet a proper city, just an outpost on the edge of endless forest.

"Well, I hope you enjoy your visit. There's a lovely wildness to the trees here." The lady smiled and then turned back to her companion.

Jamison went back to thinking about the letter. The San Francisco office said there were two purposes for the trip: to confer with the leadership of the Puget Mill Company regarding unionizing efforts and to interview a new possible recruit for the Pinkerton agency.

This Mr. Reagan lives right in the small lumber town. It would be simple to set him up as an undercover source, since he already knows the territory. What a stroke of good fortune. If he works out, that is.

Jamison closed his eyes. He felt a surge as the boat plowed a route through the restless waters. The hum of people talking made his eyes heavy. *This trip could solve our problem of how to place an agent in a small town without fanfare. And I will have a trip into the wilds as a bonus.* His head bobbed forward. He jerked awake and sat straighter. He looked at his pocket watch. Only 7:08 a.m.!

Outside, clouds shrouded the forests. The *Nora* followed close to the eastern shoreline.

The forest shoves its way up through the mist. Impressive! Massive.

The gigantic trees grew thickly down to the shoreline in most places. Here and there a tree with peeling orange bark curved out, showing its olive-green skin underneath. There was a lot of traffic in the estuary: boats with billowing sails plowing along with cargo to deliver, fishing boats, slow-moving log booms and steam passenger boats like the *Nora*.

The boat passed by a rock-strewn beach stretched out into the steel-gray waters. Another thin ribbon of sand held a jumble of sea-tossed logs and roots. But at least twice, Jamison saw open patches of land blistered with stumps.

Now, that's a sign of progress.

After staring back at the looming green draperies of forest on each side, Jamison felt a rising agitation. Sweat dotted his brow. He curled himself into a lump.

A man could feel hemmed in by giants here!

Now the boat moved out into the channel and closer to the other side. Jamison forced himself to look elsewhere. As the *Nora* made its way across the waters, he scanned the horizon. Through a break in the clouds, he saw a giant white cone of a mountain to the north. Jamison caught his breath.

"That's Mount Baker, sir," said the lady next to him. "And when we pull up to the Kingston dock, you might see the tips of the Olympic Mountains above the treetops."

"It's certainly an impressive sight, madam. Thank you for the information." He nodded and continued his observations. The boat turned westward and hummed ahead.

"Kingston," shouted a crewman. He wore a uniform with two rows of brass buttons cascading down the front.

"We'll stop a few minutes while passengers go ashore and a few supplies are unloaded. Other passengers remain aboard, please." Jamison, who wore a closely tailored wool suit, noticed one button was missing on the man's uniform. He checked his own.

A tangle of shacks and cabins popped up along the Kingston shore. Behind the village, an open patch of stumps scarred the pristine wilderness. There seemed to be no town center. A dirt road led up from the dock to a single restaurant, a ticket office and what appeared to be a post office. Two women and a man stepped off the boat carrying satchels and bags. One of the women held a child on her hip. They walked the muddy street and called out to someone. Jamison turned his gaze to the men unloading crates of potatoes, carrots and cabbages.

Does this happen at every stop? I'm glad I'm not riding to the very end!

Presently, a few new passengers boarded, and the boat backed out and turned its bow north again. The weak winter sun peeked its face over the treetops. The curtain of mist parted and then dispersed. As the boat's cabin warmed, people unwrapped their shawls and unbuttoned their suit jackets. People started chatting with each other. The sun sparkled on the wave tips like sand-polished agates in a tidal pool.

The next leg of the trip would get him to Port Gamble. Jamison walked out the door and found a place along the boat's raised rail. A wind gust raked cold fingers through his hair. He grabbed for his hat, but it wasn't on his head. He gulped a deep breath.

Ah--creosote and salt water, all part of the northwest experience.

Bracing wind, and the ancient trees watch and wait.

Here I am, making up poetry. This landscape is magnificent.

Out in the bay ahead of the *Nora*, a brown head bobbed to the surface. Jamison looked for a long time at the antics of this sea animal, a seal, which he'd seen in San Francisco Bay before, surfacing for air then diving down again for several minutes. Once it had a fish in its mouth. The fish struggled, but the seal prevailed and swallowed it down.

That suggestion of food made Jamison's stomach gurgle. Time had passed while he stood at the rail. The boat made its way toward what looked like a larger channel. As they moved into it, Jamison could see a wide strait of water. In this blue highway he looked at both shorelines and the dots of land jutting out in irregular patterns. Here, several boats passed by with a toot of the horn.

And some black creatures with distinctive white markings sped through the water nearby, small whales in evening attire.

Soon, the *Nora* passed a narrow spit of land and then made a sharp turn south, he calculated. The passage narrowed and the wind died down. Jamison shivered.

We must be almost there.

He saw buildings and heard noise—a mill. The first mate came on deck and entered the passenger area.

"Port Gamble, ladies and gentlemen. Please gather your things. We'll put up at the dock shortly."

Jamison stepped through the door and fetched his hat from the wooden bench. People inched toward the narrow deck, clutching bags and children's hands.

"We'll stop here one hour or so. Those who want some dinner can head over to the hotel. Seaside Place has bakery items and coffee for those not so hungry. We'll blow the boat's whistle when it's time to go again. If this is your stop, however, it's time to disembark." The first mate removed the side rails.

Jamison found himself at the front of the line, so he swung his leg onto the dock. Noticing a young woman pushing a large cart, he stopped to speak to her.

"Excuse me, Miss, could you point out where the hotel is?"

"Right up the hill, sir. Just follow the path straight ahead." She fussed with her hair, pushing straying caramel wisps into her arrangement of hair.

"Are you here for a certain purpose, sir?" she said. "You don't look like a new worker with that tailored suit."

"I'm curious if you know a certain person. I came to see—A. Reagan. You seem to live here and know the place." The young woman stared and put a hand up to her mouth. She hesitated before speaking.

"Was Reagan expecting you?"

"No, I came unannounced because of a letter I received just yesterday. Would you be so kind as to help me locate him?" Jamison tipped his hat toward her.

"I will, sir. Where do you want to meet Reagan? I'll take a message."

"I have a meeting with some of the managers soon after I get off the boat. But first, I'd like a meal as soon as possible. So, tell Reagan to meet me in the hotel lobby at about five o'clock. Is that possible?"

"Yes, sir. That should be fine. I'll make sure that happens." She waved and turned to her task—getting some crates off the *Nora*.

Jamison followed her directions, arriving at the

small but neat hotel. He spoke to the clerk and then found his room. He followed the aromas of cooking to the dining hall. Not elegant, but the food was ample and delicious. Just as he was finishing, two well-dressed men entered the dining room and looked around. Jamison set his lips in a thin line and waited.

Chapter 10

The man with a black beard approached Jamison. He wore his authority like a mantle. Taking out a pocket watch, he checked the time. Then he spoke.

"See here, sir," he said. "Did you just arrive on the *Nora*?" His whiskers grew like the forest outside, jammed together and untamable. His eyebrows were two shingles of moss. Outside, the *Nora's* whistle announced it was about to leave. The man shifted his polished shoes.

"Yes, sir. I left Seattle this morning. Had a pleasant trip through the sound." Jamison stood up. "I'm waiting for a meeting with Mr. Ames and Mr. Smith this afternoon. They said they'd find me. Is that why you inquired?" Jamison wiped his mouth with the linen napkin he'd retrieved from his lap.

"Smith is the name." The man held out a calloused hand. Jamison accepted it. "Sorry to disturb your dinner. Will you join us at Mr. Ames' house, where we can talk in private?" It was a command, not a question. He turned and made for the entry where another man waited. Jamison buttoned his coat, dropped some coins on the table and followed. After meeting a robust Mr. Ames, the three men left.

"Come next door, Jamison."

Mr. Ames took long strides toward the nicest house by far Jamison had seen in Port Gamble. It stood two stories high. Jamison counted more than a dozen glass windowpanes on it. The grand entry door faced the bay rather than Rainier Avenue, like the other buildings, but the rest of the house faced the bay.

"I like to watch for the ships coming into Gamble Bay. Then, I invite the captains and business agents to my home for dinner. It's just good business," said Ames. "I'm the manager of Puget Mill Company. We trade with ports in San Francisco, and also the Orient—Hawaii, Shanghai and Singapore and others. Our lumber has found its way around the world."

The three men strode up a few stairs and into a wide entrance hall. The floors shone with polish. Large ferns cascaded over cloisonné china bowls set on plant stands. Another tall pot on the floor held several umbrellas. A round table in the middle of the foyer contained a large arrangement of fragrant evergreen branches. Mr. Ames led the others directly to his study. On the way they stepped on densely woven oriental rugs of rust and navy. A grandfather clock ticked, swinging its pendulum rhythmically.

The study smelled of stale cigars. Jamison held

back a cough. Mr. Ames motioned for them to sit. Two fine horsehair couches stood at right angles to the fireplace that crackled with its pitchy logs just catching fire. A large silver tray held all the necessities for coffee.

"Gentlemen, please help yourselves. My wife tells me we have some nut breads from our own bakery, Seaside Place." Smith and Jamison in turn filled a plate with the savory breads and got a steaming cup of coffee.

"Mr. Jamison, my name is Edwin Ames. I was hired by the owners to steer the Puget Mill Company and keep it on a sound economic course. If you looked around you as you came here, you'll see there are unlimited resources to be used." Mr. Jamison nodded and took a sip from his cup.

"An impressive opportunity, sir," he said.

"That's why we need to proceed without hindrance," said Ames. "Mr. Smith here has done an admirable job of acquiring tracts of timber. We need to have a steady supply because we run the saws twenty-four hours a day. We have two eleven and a half-hour shifts. If you stay here any amount of time, you'll get used to the buzz of the saws. Why, for me, I listen to the hum as I fall asleep at night. It's like a lullaby." The great man stopped pacing and shoved his hands in his pockets. Jamison joined Smith in laughing at the older man's joke.

"How may I help?"

"We have a problem here, Jamison." Ames cut in. "The men are no longer content to do their shifts. Many quit because they fear falling victim to the open blades. Shirkers are replaced quickly enough by fresh workers, of course, but now, there are rumors the men want higher wages." Ames slammed his fist on the thick mahogany table. Smith jerked and spilled a drop of coffee on the sofa.

"We can't have work stoppages. We can't afford to pay more. We must hold the line on costs!" Jamison sat up straighter to catch every word.

Ames' face had taken on a purplish tinge. He sat down in a side chair with a slump. Seeing this, Mr. Smith took up the conversation thread.

"We've called you here to investigate, Jamison. Look into the whole situation. Who are the instigators? Who's pushing for reforms? Who's the loudest voice? The biggest troublemaker?" He paused and sipped his coffee.

"Get to the heart of the problem, as fast as you can," said Ames. "Report back to me as soon as possible. We'll need to take steps to correct the problem before production is seriously slowed."

"Let me be very clear. We have no intention of bowing to any conditions," roared Mr. Ames. "We just need to develop a strategy to rid ourselves of labor agitators. They stir up unrest, things the men never even thought of before."

"I see, sir," said Jamison. "Pinkerton will

insinuate itself into the life of Port Gamble and investigate. We'll listen to every conversation and argument. We'll find out who the troublemakers are and report quickly to you, Mr. Ames." Jamison wiped his forehead with a clean handkerchief.

"That's better," said Ames. "Now that you understand, I think we can do business." Ames opened an initialed box and chose a fat cigar. He found a stick match and struck it on his shoe. With a big puff of smoke, he sat back and exhaled.

"Yes, sir. Let's do business."

Smith 's face relaxed into a smile. One gold tooth gleamed. He shoved the date nut bread into his mouth. Jamison 's whole body had tensed in the last few minutes. He had to consciously relax his tightened fists. After a few minutes discussing details and terms, he excused himself and left. On the steps outside, Jamison let out a long breath.

This will be quite an assignment.

CHAPTER 11

The loaded cart refused to move. It was caught on a tree root. Addie gave it a shove. Two boxes tumbled to the ground, with a crunching sound.

"Oh, no! The peppermint sticks." Addie set the two boxes back on the cart. She proceeded up the hill toward the general store, packages bouncing and wheels wobbling. The spicy aroma of the candy, mingled with pungent pine and fragrant juniper surrounding her, tickled her nose. She sneezed.

Her father met her at the door and helped her push the cart inside the store.

"I've been waiting a long time for these supplies." He checked all the boxes and barrels against his order list. "What happened to these?" He pointed to the crumpled boxes.

"They fell." Addie avoided his eyes.

"Be more careful or I'll dock your pay, daughter."

"Father, I'll help you stock the shelves." Addie took some containers of baking powder and set them on the display shelf. Next, small bottles of cinnamon and ginger, pepper and dried laurel leaves lined another shelf.

"Set the bag of salt on the back counter, Addie. I'll heft that big sack of flour." Potatoes, onions, cabbages and carrots found their way to various bins next.

"I'll take the bolts of cloth now," said Addie. She lifted half a dozen of them and carried the rainbow of colors toward the sewing supplies display. She banged into the counter and dropped one bolt on the floor.

"What's the rush, Addie?" said her dad.

"I have an appointment at five o'clock, Father. It's really important." She cleared her throat. "I'm applying for a job and the man doing the interview came in on the *Nora* today."

"An interview?"

"Yes, with a prestigious agency." Addie squared her shoulders and took a deep breath. "I've been wanting to tell you and Mother. With a real job, I can amount to something."

"What about finding another young man and getting married?"

"That might happen in the future, but for now I need to have a job." Addie's hands formed into fists at her sides. "I want this job, Father."

"Why didn't you tell us earlier?" Lines creased Father's forehead.

"Well, I had planned to, but this Agent Jamison arrived today—it was a surprise." Addie folded her hands together and brought them up to her chin.

"Please, if I finish my share now, could I go early and get ready for the interview?"

"If it's that important, yes." Addie's father stroked his chin whiskers. "But, don't leave until four o'clock, daughter. This is payday, so lots of people will be stopping by."

The next three hours everyone in town appeared to buy flour, spices, potatoes, stick matches—everything under the sun, it seemed. Addie and her father filled orders and took money as fast as they could, but when one customer left another walked in the door. Addie wiped her brow. Father took out his watch.

"Addie, it's time for you to go get ready. Skedaddle!" He smiled at her.

"I hate to leave you to this mob, Father," said Addie.

"Go. They'll wait their turns. You have something important to do."

Addie caught her breath. "Oh, Dad!" She threw her arms around Cameron Murray's neck.

"Your mother and I want you to succeed in life, and earning money is necessary, being as you're a single woman again." He patted her back and gave her a nudge. "Hurry now. Mother's at a quilting bee, so we'll tell her later."

Addie raced home. She took off her muddy shoes first and cleaned them with the stiff brush they kept at the back door. She heated some water and poured it into a bowl in the sink. Grabbing the soap, Addie scrubbed off the dust and dirt she'd picked up from all those boxes and burlap bags. She used a towel to blot her face and dry her hands. Then she ran up to her room.

Addie peeled off her calico shirtwaist and then the blue full skirt and let them drop to the floor. The closet door creaked as she opened it. Following the plan made between Sarah and herself, Addie undid the hook and slipped her gabardine skirt off the hanger. The folds of the skirt rustled as she stepped into them. After fastening the skirt around her waist, she reached for the basque, the closely fitted top that showed her form. She attached it to the skirt with more hooks and eyes. It was much different than the blouse she wore each day that gathered loosely across her bosom.

I hate wearing those suffocating corsets. Never again! The layers of lingerie are a bother, too. Five layers—I don't have the patience. Fortunately, I still have a slim waist and don't need to be cinched in.

Addie looked into the cheval mirror standing in the corner.

I look nice, like a young professional woman.

Addie smiled at herself for a few seconds, turning all around to see her image. A few pins plunked on the floor and her hair sagged on one side.

I'd better hurry. How much time do I have?

Addie's fingers trembled, brushing and gathering, rolling and pinning her shoulder blade long hair. When she finished, her hair looked like swirls of taffy just stirred and ready to be formed into candies. Addie ran downstairs and grabbed her boots. Her fingers labored to lace all the eyelets, but she finished and stepped out the door. She trotted all the way to the hotel. A few raindrops hit her face. Taking a deep breath, Addie counted to ten and then entered the lobby.

Mr. Jamison looked up briefly, then checked his pocket watch and scowled.

Addie bit her lip.

It's now or never.

She glided in to meet the man who would decide her future. She felt her foot catch on the Oriental rug. She paused long enough to re-position her glossy boots.

"Where's Reagan?" said Mr. Jamison. "I told you to get him here at five."

"I've come to tell you—"

"Where is he?" He tapped his foot and waited.

Addie gulped. "I'm Reagan. Addie Reagan, and I'm here for the interview."

"I reserved the library. Come with me." Mr. Jamison scratched his fair hair and gestured for her to follow him.

She stopped as they entered the library. Mr. Jamison closed the door and Addie sat opposite him on a stiff wooden chair. He leaned back in the overstuffed chair. The horsehair groaned and let out a puff of dust. He pulled out some papers from his portfolio.

"I need to hire a new man for an investigation here in Port Gamble."

"I'm not a man, but I can be your agent in this small community" Addie's words came out with quiet force. Addie looked around at the furnishings of the small library. A blue and white Chinese bowl sat on a round table by the window. It contained a giant fern. Bookcases lined two walls. The heavy tomes contained a layer of dust and the fine sawdust that forever hovered over the mill town. Several wing chairs sat in groups next to side tables where coffee and pipes could be placed. The place reeked of cigar smoke.

Addie rehearsed her ten reasons in her head:

I notice things. I live here and know almost everyone. I have a gun and I know how to shoot it. You won't have the expense of moving someone here. I'm strong, for a woman. I can learn. I—

"Miss or Mrs.?" Jamison started.

"Mrs."

"Mrs. Reagan, you lied to me about your identity." Mr. Jamison coughed.

"No, sir. I didn't. You did not require me to say male or female."

"That's true, I suppose, but I assumed you were a man."

"That is only your assumption." Addie gulped and went on. "May I remind you Pinkerton's once had a female agent who solved President Lincoln's assassination?" Addie clenched her hands in her lap.

Mr. Jamison squeezed one eye closed, while the other eyebrow shot up at a sharp angle. He paused and cracked his knuckles.

"I suppose. Let me begin again. I'm Simon Jamison, sent by Pinkerton's Detective Agency to interview you for a possible position based here at Port Gamble. We are hoping to find a person like you who is a resident and therefore could blend into the background while conducting investigations. I have a few questions to ask you." He shifted his legs.

"Your inquiry tells very little about yourself, so describe to me your qualifications."

"I am nineteen years old and widowed. I own a modified Colt 1851 Navy revolver."

"Can you shoot it?" said Jamison. "It's heavy for a woman."

"Yes, I've practiced loading and shooting it. Of course, I do hope to get a smaller weapon after I save some money. But I am strong. I work in the general store lifting large sacks of potatoes, flour and onions regularly."

"What qualifies you to be an agent?"

"I notice things. I once solved a mystery here at Port Gamble—Mrs. Smith's pearl necklace went missing and I followed the clues to recover it."

"I see. Anything else to recommend yourself?"

Jamison smoothed his mustache with one stroke on each side.

"I can move around town invisibly. Everyone knows me, so no one will suspect I'm watching them."

"Yes?"

"And I can learn quickly. I'm eager to better myself. You won't be disappointed if you hire me."

"Tell me about your husband. Does he approve of your applying for a job?" Jamison inclined his head slightly.

"He was killed in a mill accident."

"How did it happen?"

"I don't know many details, just what I was told. Sam worked the big saw that day and, somehow, he caught his suspenders in it. He was pushing in one of the giant logs, you know."

"Yes, and what happened to him?"

"He was pulled into the saw and sliced like a piece of wood." Addie's voice came out as a hoarse rasp. "I only saw his bloody hand when I got there." She stifled a sob and covered her eyes.

"Perhaps you are becoming an agent to investigate your husband's death?"

Addie looked at her hands. "I hadn't thought of that till now." Jamison raised an eyebrow.

"Do you believe in right and wrong, Mrs. Reagan?"

"Of course."

"Why is it important to catch criminals? For revenge?"

"Not just that. To preserve order in our society, to protect people from injury and death, and most importantly, to uphold God's justice."

"Well said. A very proper answer." Agent Jamison cleared his throat and shuffled his papers into a neat pile. "As I said, we need an agent soon. Should you be the one chosen?"

Addie leaned forward, waiting for the next words out of Agent Jamison's mouth.

My future depends on it, sir.

CHAPTER 12

Mr. Jamison got up and walked around the library. Addie picked at her short fingernails. She slid one finger around the high collar of her dress. Sweat drops popped out on her forehead. Addie stood up and strode to the window. Outside, a thin mist trickled down from the gray sky. She spotted a Northern flicker fly up into a tree, its black-striped back and spotted breast dazzling to the eyes. Only a few people moved around on Port Gamble's grounds. To get soaked in January could bring on a cold and worse. Addie turned around as a log in the fire crackled and shifted. She composed her skirts and trembling hands.

I will believe and not doubt! That's what Pastor Deming said.

Mr. Jamison stood with his back facing Addie, his head bowed. Minutes passed with the ticking of the clock on the mantel. Addie whispered, *please, please.* At last, he turned and returned to the horsehair chair. He fussed with the lacy antimacassar that lined the top of the chair, and then adjusted his tie.

"Mrs. Reagan, I've come to a decision."

"Yes?"

"I will hire you, but, with some conditions."

Addie gasped and clapped her hands together.

"You have very little experience and training, but I'll take you on probation. The need here is urgent, and you can begin at once, I assume."

"Yes. I'm ready." Addie bobbed her head several times.

"Very well. I will hire you for ninety days. You must prove your worth by then or I will be forced to look elsewhere. Do you understand?" He scowled.

"Thank you, a thousand times, Mr. Jamison," said Addie. "I understand the arrangement. I promise I won't disappoint you. What's the assignment? What are my duties and what is expected of me?"

"Good. Right to business, I see," said Jamison. "You can begin tomorrow, that will be fine. Let me explain terms and duties, too. We'll give you a small stipend for incidental expenses. Your salary will be paid on the first of each month." Jamison took an envelope out of his portfolio and withdrew one crisp ten-dollar bill. "Here, take this for expenses, though I doubt you'll have many in this small town."

Addie took the bill and put it in her skirt pocket. Outside, the sun painted a rainbow on the other side of the lawn. Addie felt a warm glow inside as she saw the airy wonder. Then, she settled back to listen to Mr. Jamison. He explained the terms so well even Sarah would be satisfied.

Agent Jamison went on to explain the situation at Port Gamble and the problem to be found out. Her smile disappeared. Much later, Addie bade good-bye to Mr. Jamison and left the hotel. Informed and armed, as her new boss said, she walked home. It was dark now, but no rain pelted her.

Will Mother be mad I missed supper? Will she approve of her new career?

Addie trotted the rest of the way to her parents' home with the news.

"Addie, come in and get warm! Goodness, where is your sense? No shawl?" Her mother fussed around her and went to the stove. "I saved some soup for you."

"I'm sorry, Mother, I had an appointment at five. I hope Father mentioned it."

"He did."

"Mr. Jamison wanted to do some training afterward." Addie looked at her father as he ambled in. "I got hired!"

"That's wonderful, Addie. We are proud of you." He patted her back.

"That's very well, Addie, but I, for one, do not approve," said her mother. "Being a detective is a man's job, plain and simple. It's not for a proper lady."

"I was desperate, Mother. There are no opportunities here in Port Gamble. Unless you can chop trees or mill wood." Addie threw up her hands.

"Don't be impertinent. And I don't see why you, Cameron, are so interested in our daughter associating with criminals and low-life scoundrels every day."

"Caroline. Don't you see? Addie needs to find her way. She doesn't want to tend the general store forever. Do you, Addie?"

"No, Father. I want to do something important with my life. I want to make a difference, and I think this is how." She looked at her mother and added:

"Unfortunately, Mr. Jamison didn't hire me, Mother. So, I've decided to write a book about Port Gamble, instead. You know, a bit of history and some description of the landscape." Mr. Murray raised an eyebrow and was about to say something. Addie shook her head.

"Humph." Her mother turned away. "I did the dishes tonight, Addie, but I expect you to be here tomorrow. This writing must not interfere with your family duties." She walked out of the kitchen.

Cameron Murray looked at his daughter. "Well, it's a start, Addie. I'm proud of you. Keep following your path. You're creating a new life for yourself and I applaud you." He put his arms around Addie and gave her a hug.

"And I'll keep your secret from your mother.

I think we both agree she would not keep your secret. It's not in her nature."

"Thank you, Father. I'll make you proud of me. Good night." They trudged up the stairs and parted on the landing to their different rooms.

In her room, Addie couldn't stop smiling until she started thinking what she'd have to do on this new job. Agent Jamison said to make discrete inquiries and use her noticing skills to root out the labor agitators from among the mill workers.

That part won't be too hard. I know most of them, already. What could be done about the other problem?

Some people suspected somebody was illegally claiming tracts of timber without paying for them. It wasn't as if the timberlands were expensive. It was the inconvenience. And land commissioners sometimes looked the other way, Addie knew, because of the forest itself.

The nine-foot diameter trees grew thickly, blocking out the sun, and making it impossible to find a way through the groves. In fact, it was so clogged with roots that the inspectors couldn't wedge a foot inside the untouched land. How would loggers get in there with their long saws? How would the trees even find a place to fall when severed from their roots? How could the land commissioners assess the value of the tracts?

I live at Port Gamble. That's a plus, but I'm a woman. That will make me noticeable and suspicious if I spend any time around the mill. How will I arrest the wrongdoers when the time comes? I've got to practice again with that pistol, somewhere where I won't be noticed or heard.

Addie hung up her good black skirt and top on a hook in the tiny closet. She braided her hair into one loose strand and slipped the nightgown over her head. As she settled in bed, she said again as her evening prayer,

Help me believe and not doubt tomorrow.

Chapter 13

"Why aren't you slackers working yet?"

Jake Hardy, mill foreman, stormed into the mill looking for someone to pick on. At five minutes before six in the morning, most men had hung up their jackets on a nail and rolled up their sleeves. But the whistle hadn't blown yet. One or two stragglers raced in to meet the deadline and be on the job on time.

"Power up the saws, Johnson. You six men roll the first log onto the belt. It's time to make money for our bosses."

The men moved slowly, still full of sleep and a warm bed. But the day shift was beginning, and so they must join the grand scheme of producing perfectly planed and cured boards to be shipped to San Francisco, Shanghai, Singapore, Hawaii and Australia.

Hardy was a hard man, pushing and prodding to get higher production from the workers. He was proud Puget Mill had the highest production of any mill in the territory. The men worked eleven and a half hours, only pausing that half hour to run to the dining hall and shovel in a meal of boiled corn beef, potatoes, baked beans, hash, hot griddle cakes and coffee.

In one sense, it was a great opportunity to work for Puget Mill. The pay was good, thirty dollars a month. Every week they got paid with a stack of fifty-cent pieces. Some would go home to help the family. Some would stay here so a man could enjoy an occasional sarsaparilla or purchase a new pair of woolen socks.

The company store could supply almost anything and the big bosses, Pope and Talbot, kept them contented with entertainments, socials, competing on baseball teams in the summer, even musical events. They banned gambling and bad women, and even let a man bring his family out here to the wildness of Washington Territory. But Jake Hardy flexed his muscles and his will, always striving to make the mill profitable.

And men were dying.

The whistle blew and Hardy got the shift moving.

"Come on, boys. Let's see your muscle. Push those logs through! "Hardy walked up and down the line urging them to work faster. If a man couldn't take the pressure, he quit. But right behind him a new man got hired.

"Move, move, move!"

The oscillating sash saw screamed as a well-muscled man pushed the squared log through, slicing another board. At the other end, Chen Fu lifted and stacked the board on the growing pile before the next one came through. Eddie George worked his way through the aisle, pushing a wide broom. The sawdust must not pile up anywhere. Sparks from the machinery could easily ignite a fire.

"Hey, Chen, did you go to the social Friday?" asked Eddie. The saw whined on.

Chen Fu cupped a hand to his ear and shook his head. He pulled out another board. Every day the same motions, the same thing over and over.

"We talk at lunch, okay?" Eddie yelled. Chen nodded and continued his work.

Hardy talked for a moment to Tony Esposito, who curled his lip and laughed. Everyone knew Hardy sometimes left in the middle of shift to go see Mr. Smith. That was when Tony took over. He had a cruel streak and didn't mind elbowing a worker who didn't respond quickly. Those shoves sent a man within inches of the screaming blades of the giant saws. Or, Tony might knock down a pile of lumber and make the worker re-stack it double fast. Most of all, he loved to rough up the labor agitators.

Tony drew close to Chen Fu's workspace on his way toward the door.

"I don't suppose you understand me, do you, Chinaman?"

Chen gave him a blank look and kept working.

"That's what I thought." Tony laughed. "I

guess I could say anything in your presence then, couldn't I? I could say I'm going to see Mr. Smith about the tract of land he procured—or stole—about getting the logs cut into lumber as soon as possible before a land commissioner hears about it. What do you think of that?" Tony chuckled as Chen shrugged his shoulders. Tony walked down the line to see to the other workers.

Jake Hardy, the foreman, strode over to Elliot Smith's house on executive row and rapped on the door. A maid answered and ushered him in. Hardy stepped up to the study door and tapped twice.

"Come in, Hardy." Mr. Smith's voiced boomed. Jake came in, hat in hand.

"I've got a couple of log rafts coming in tonight with those logs I told you about. Came from a tract across the Sound. I took them while George Brackett's back was turned. He's just setting up his claim. I need to get the logs sawn into boards quickly. If George sets the land commissioners on me, I don't want the lumber identified as coming from there."

"I understand, Mr. Smith. What do you need me to do?"

"Get the night shift to work on them as soon as they appear. The sooner the better."

"I'll see it gets done. Anything else?

"That's it. You can go." Smith turned his back and shuffled papers on his desk.

"Right." Jake exited in long strides and closed the door lightly behind him. He heard a noise in the hall, a small gasp, and looked around. Not seeing anyone, he left without waiting for someone to show him out. He'd be pulling two shifts today.

CHAPTER 14

Addie walked over to Marianne Smith's house on Monday night to practice a piano duet with her. They had promised to perform Schubert's "Serenade" for the Friday night social. Mrs. Smith let her in. Addie clutched her worn piano book.

"Hello, Addie. Thank you for agreeing to perform with Marianne on Friday. We must keep encouraging her to develop her musical skills." She drew up her ample bosom.

"It's good for me, as well, Mrs. Smith. There aren't enough opportunities to hear classical music out here in the forests, are there?" She smiled at Marianne, who waited in the parlor.

"Well, take off your coat and come right this way." She took Addie's wrap and ushered her toward the piano. "Did you have time to practice?"

"I'm sorry, we don't have a piano, so whenever I can, I sneak over to the hall and use that one."

"Well, come along. Perhaps you'll put in extra time this week, both of you. I'm sure you want a flawless performance on Friday."

"Yes, ma'am. Hello, Marianne." Addie sat down

at the piano, opening her piano book to the right pages.

"Hullo." Marianne plunked down beside her. They raised their hands to the right keys. "Let's try to play it all the way through without stopping."

"All right. One, two, three—" They each came in at their appointed times and made it to the middle before Marianne faltered. "Oh, I just can't do this part," she said, dropping her hands into her lap.

"Keep going anyway," said Addie, and kept up her part. Marianne missed a few beats, but her fingers touched the right keys again. They labored to the end and then let out a laugh.

"We did it," they said together.

"I see possibilities," said Mrs. Smith as she entered the room clapping. "Do it a few more times, and why don't you come over Thursday night for dinner. You can do one final practice session." Marianne wriggled her nose.

"That's very nice, Mrs. Smith. It's a good idea. I'd love to come to dinner. Just name the time."

"Six o'clock sharp. Mr. Smith demands promptness."

"I'll be here. Again, thank you."

Marianne and Addie practiced some of the ragged parts and then ran through the piece a few more times. After that, Addie decided she had stayed a bit too long. Mrs. Smith was pacing the floor, wringing her hands, and Marianne kept fluffing her skirts.

"Good night, Mrs. Smith," Addie said as she put on her coat and grabbed her book. "I'll practice every day this week till Thursday. We'll do our very best."

"I assure you Marianne will do her part, as well. Good night."

Addie looked up the stairs and noticed Marcus Williams standing at the top. He raised his hands and made silent clapping motions. Addie's cheeks burned, but she gave him the smallest of smiles in return. He disappeared before Mrs. Smith glanced that way. Addie ran all the way home through the dark, rainy night.

Next day, she worked in the general store helping her father clean the shelves and sweep the floors. Sawdust from the mill continually found its way into every crevice. After that chore, Addie tried something new.

"Father, let me arrange all the sewing items in an attractive display. I know ladies would like that." He nodded from his desk. Addie found several baskets and put buttons in one, thimbles and needle packets in another and scissors in the third. She placed them all on a remnant of blue calico folded in waves. Then she printed a small sign telling the prices of each item and set a sewing box next to it all.

"Very nice, Addie," said her father from his

desk. "I sure hope nobody helps themselves to the buttons."

"Not the ladies of Port Gamble!"

"I suppose you're right. Now, you wanted to practice the piano for a while? Go ahead. It's not busy here."

Addie waved to her father and took her music book. Across the street, she entered the community hall and found the piano. She quickly lost herself in the music and didn't hear the creak of the wood floor.

Somebody started clapping. She started and turned around. Tony Esposito! He slowly walked toward her. His meaty hands made the clapping fill the room and bounce off the walls.

"So, you play the piano, Addie. Nice." Addie stood up and stepped away from the piano bench.

Tony sidled up to her and pulled her chin toward his line of sight. "What other talents can you show me?" She held as still and cold as a side of beef in a meat locker, but met his gaze.

"Shouldn't you be working?" she said. He looked away and plunked a few notes on the piano keys. His laugh came in staccato bursts, like bullets hitting her.

"Have a good day, Addie Reagan." Tony sauntered out of the empty hall.

After he was gone, Addie grabbed her book and ran back to the store. She went to the sink in back and washed her hands with strong soap.

By Thursday night, Addie had mastered her part. She put on her new shirtwaist and smoothed her hair before walking over to the Smiths' house. She hadn't heard the stop whistle yet, so she knew she was early. She was surprised to see Marcus at the table.

The dinner was delicious: roasted chicken with mashed potatoes and gravy flavored with mushrooms. Cochran picked out the mushrooms. Marianne picked at her food and leaned on one elbow. Mrs. Smith ignored her and had the dessert served, a delicate apple tart with a mound of whipped cream. Soon, Mr. Smith excused himself and went to his study.

Practice went well. Marianne had prepared. Addie and Marianne played the piece through perfectly the first time. They did it once more. Addie excused herself; Marianne swished her way out of the parlor. Marcus stifled a smile as he stood discreetly in the hall.

"I hope to see you tomorrow, Miss Reagan," he said, bowing slightly, hands behind him.

"I'll be there, Mr. Williams."

"Well, good night."

Addie pulled her shawl around her. The moon shone in each drop of dew settled on the green bit of lawn on executive row. It was a singular evening.

Friday night arrived. Addie wore her girly dress, a sage green calico with a white lace collar and puffed sleeves. She brushed her hair and tied a rose-colored ribbon in it. Outside, people streamed toward the community hall. Addie took a seat in the second row. Other performers had filled the first row already. She left a place next to her on the aisle. A minute later, Marcus slipped into the seat and smiled.

"I'm anxious to witness your performance tonight, Addie."

"I'm playing with her. It's a duet, Mr. Williams." Marianne turned around and leaned toward him.

"Shh," said Addie. "It's time to start." Mr. Ames, the manager of the whole town, stepped up on stage and made a few remarks. Then, it was time for their duet. They were first on the program.

"Watch out, Addie," said Marianne as she slid onto the piano bench. She narrowed her eyes and stuck out her tongue.

"Let's get started," Addie whispered back. Their fingers flowed over the keys. Marianne clearly had some talent and had applied herself. Addie enjoyed her moment on the stage and then bowed for the applause and got off the stage quickly.

Marcus touched her hand with a brief squeeze. Marianne's program dropped to the floor. Marcus leaned forward to pick it up. Marianne raised her eyebrows at Addie.

After the program, Marianne and Cochran crowded around Marcus and asked a lot of questions. Addie got a cup of tea, ate a piece of gingerbread and left.

"Walk with us, daughter. It's safer." Cameron Murray drew up to Addie with his wife on his arm. They strolled in the indigo murk of a February night.

"You did well, Addie," said her mother. "Of course, the tempo was a bit slow."

They sauntered to their home and Addie went right up to bed.

Addie sobbed into her pillow.

I miss you, Sam.

CHAPTER 15

On Sunday, Addie sat in church in the second pew back, alongside her parents. She could see the beads of perspiration on Mrs. Deming's forehead as she played the piano for the singing. Last week, Pastor Deming spoke about not doubting and asking for wisdom. Today he was a different person. He stepped up to the lectern with heavy feet and gripped its edges till his knuckles turned white.

"I tell you, do not think you will escape God's wrath. He cannot abide sin of any kind. He has prepared a place, a horrible pit for each one of us. Confess your sin and God may pluck you from the region of the Devil." He pounded the pulpit and took a breath. A silly giggle escaped his mouth.

Addie took it all in. She heard pews creak throughout the small church as the congregants leaned back, pinned by the force of the pastor's words.

What happened to 'Believe and not doubt?' I remember Pastor Deming's comforting words at Sam's funeral last year. He said, 'God is near the brokenhearted,' that weeping may endure for a time, but joy will come.

God prepares a place for all believers in his heavenly home. But now, the pastor was all wrath and destruction!

Pastor Deming continued for another forty minutes, spelling out in vivid detail the plight of sinners and an angry God. Addie had heard of a preacher named Jonathan Edwards who had preached along those lines early in the country's history, but this was new for Pastor Deming. The air was still as a graveyard. A baby in the back wailed, but the mother silenced it quickly. Addie sat close enough to see Pastor Deming's face. His cheeks were rosy and his nose a deep purple. His eyes looked strange, with red streaks traversing the whites. Even though his words were harsh, his face conveyed a sense of deep rapture. He was jubilant! He looked to be bursting with energy.

This is all wrong. He's always been a gentle man.

"In closing, let me say—" Pastor Deming paused. A vacant look filled his eyes. He gripped the pulpit. Mrs. Deming looked at him with an uncertain expression. An awkward pause passed, then Mrs. Deming took action. She signaled the last hymn with forceful piano chords. Pastor Deming slumped down heavily in the chair on the podium. The church cleared out faster than closing time at the mill, and everyone headed home without so much as a word to anyone. Everyone except Addie. She sat there quietly watching the aftermath of the morning's sermon.

She noticed Mary Deming close the lid on

the piano keys and surge toward her husband. He sat slumped over, eyes closed in the chair on the podium. A little drama played out as Addie squirmed in her seat.

"John, are you all right?" Mary took his hand and patted it. He opened one eye. It must have looked odd, because she recoiled as if bitten by a snake.

"Why, yes, dear. I'm perfectly fine," he said. Addie was close enough to hear his words slur together. The next moment his eyes shut. "Just let me rest here a moment and I'll be ready to go home."

"I'll go greet the people at the door, John." Mary walked out the back door to meet the congregation. Addie craned her neck to the rear. All she saw were the backs of the people, receding like the tide. She saw Mary, the pastor's wife, frown and wring her hands. Mary grabbed a broom and swept vigorously down the aisles, till dust rose in a swirling cloud.

Addie stood and began straightening hymnbooks and picking up dropped bulletins. She grabbed a cloth and dusted the display table, as well as the lectern. She avoided disturbing Pastor Deming, but Mary looked up. After resting the broom in the back alcove, she walked forward. She acknowledged Addie with a hand on her arm. Addie gave her a hug. Just then, Pastor Deming roused, wiped his face with a handkerchief and adjusted his vest. He lifted himself out of the chair and stepped off the platform.

"I believe I'm ready to go home now, Mary. Are you ready?"

"I'm coming, John. Let me take your arm." Mary grabbed his wool-clad limb with both hands and supported him as he lumbered home. She flashed a smile at Addie, and then turned her full attention to her husband.

"John, why did you deliver such a scalding sermon today? It's not like you." She looked at his profile from her vantage point.

"Never mind, Mary. The deacons demanded last week that I preach the fear of God's wrath to the congregation. I find it harsh, but there it is. I had to gather my courage this morning." He sighed.

"You seemed possessed by a greater power today, that is for certain. You alarmed me, and I think others, too." She squeezed his arm.

"One Sunday at a time, Mary. We'll succeed here by satisfying the deacons." John gnashed his teeth together and jutted out his chin.

"I hope you're right, dear. Now, let's get home and eat a little lunch."

Addie mouthed to her, "Let's have tea tomorrow." Mary nodded.

Addie walked home and heard nothing else that day. She pondered the strange happenings, burying them deep in her heart. She made a note to watch the pastor's behavior closely and find out what motivated him. *What secret tormented him?*

Addie sent a note to Mary Deming that afternoon inviting her to meet for tea at Seaside Place. It wasn't the most private of places. It was a busy bakery and meeting place. But there were quiet corners and Addie needed to talk to the pastor's wife.

The next day Addie waved to Mary Deming as she stepped into the spicy- scented ambience of Seaside Place.

"Hi, Mary. Come and sit with me. I've ordered a pot of tea and some scones." Mary joined her at a corner table. A large plant obscured them from view.

"Thanks for coming, Mary. I thought you'd enjoy an afternoon break with me." She poured strong tea into two sturdy cups and offered her some lemon scones.

"It's kind of you to invite me, Addie. I don't often go out during the day just for enjoyment."

"I feel the same way. I usually work all day at the general store, to help my father."

"What did you want to talk about?" Mary took a sip of the tea and set it down on the saucer with a shaky hand. She broke off a corner of the scone and popped it into her mouth.

"We've been friends a long time, haven't we?" Addie smiled at Mary.

"Of course."

"When I lost Sam, you let me cry over thousands of cups of coffee in your kitchen. There was nobody I could pour my heart out but to you. Thank you." Addie leaned over and squeezed Mary's hand.

"That's what friends are for, dear one." Mary grabbed Addie's other hand.

"And when I lost my baby—I wanted to die." Addie choked back a sob.

"Glad to listen, glad to comfort— It took a lot of months to see hope return to your eye. What's this all about?" Mary's eyes held questions.

"If you don't mind my boldness, friend, I noticed yesterday that your husband acted strangely when he preached. I've never seen him like that. I thought maybe he was sick or maybe disturbed about something. Is he all right?" Addie searched Mary's eyes.

Mary flinched and drew back slightly.

"I'm not sure I understand what you mean, Addie."

"He seemed a bit unsteady on his feet and lost his train of thought sometimes. I don't mean to be nosy and anything you say, I would never repeat anything to anyone. I just want to know if I can help in any way."

Mary shuddered and gulped some air.

"Oh, Addie. I don't know what to do. John is

acting in such an odd manner these days. He stays up late to study his commentaries, he says, but I think he might be— drinking." She whispered the last word.

"Do you smell alcohol on his breath?"

"No, just the faintest sweet smell comes from his clothing. It's enticing."

"Enticing? In what way?"

"You want to smell the aroma yourself and sink into a trance. What am I to do? Whatever John is doing is clearly out of bounds." Mary Deming covered her eyes.

"Have you ever seen the source of this sweet smell?" Addie reached out and patted Mary's shoulder.

"No, I have no idea what this thing is that has caught hold of my husband, but I'm afraid. It could cost him his job—and his reputation." Mary's eyes got big. "Please don't mention it to anyone—not ever. Promise me."

"I do promise," said Addie. "But you promise me something, too. If you have any more problems or need someone to talk to, please let me know. I'm happy to listen."

Mary nodded, tears filling her eyes. She sat a minute more to compose herself. She finished her scone, nodded to Addie and slipped away. Addie watched and wondered.

CHAPTER 16

Things were changing for Addie. Since she got hired two weeks ago by Pinkerton's agency, she had attended a musical recital, a book club and a political discussion meeting. She'd also become more visible on Port Gamble's streets. All this was to search for clues in the bits of conversation she overheard everywhere. Addie hardly had time to help her father at the store anymore. But she decided to keep working part-time to keep things appearing normal.

But all was not normal. The political meeting started out as a gathering of mill workers and their families. She brought a pot of baked beans and sat down with people who had been Sam's friends. Ben and Leah Banks were having a baby. Jim Scranton was bringing his family from Maine to Port Gamble. And George Frederick, well, he just flirted with Addie.

"Addie, will you come watch me play baseball this spring?" He leaned forward on his elbows, his hands holding up his chin. "The team's good this year. In fact, it's improved every year since it started over ten years ago."

"Of course, George. I like baseball. I'm sure I'll be there sometimes." Addie finished the last bit of fried chicken off her plate and wiped her hands.

"But, will you come and root for me? I'm a real good hitter." He flexed a bicep.

"Now, George, why are you bothering Addie?" said Ben. "Sam's only been gone barely a year. She's still a grieving widow."

"Sorry, Addie, but maybe by April or May will you be ready to think about me—me and you?" George was a penitent but eager puppy.

"George, you're a good friend. I need to leave it that way for now." Addie gave him a smile. "I've got to be going," she started to say, but a discussion at the next table got loud and angry.

"You know the bosses don't care if we get hurt in the mills, Reuben. To them, it's all about profit," said a man with a purple face. "Admit it!"

"Now, Harry, calm down. We're working for better conditions. We should just slow down our production till we feel we can work safely." Reuben waved his large, callused hands.

"Yeah, and get fired," said Harry.

"Well, why not quit then?"

"That does no good and you know it. There's a long line of men waiting to take your job if you step away."

Harry stood up. "How many of you men want a safer place to work?" A number of hands went up amid lots of muttering.

"How about higher wages? That's what I really want," said Ben, jumping to his feet. "We're having a baby." He motioned to his wife, Leah, who looked pink around the ears. Some of the ladies oohed and a few men clapped.

"Don't let Hardy hear you—or Tony, either. You may end up in the grinder." Harry jabbed his finger in the air.

That's crazy. Pope and Talbot treat us pretty good." Ben sat down.

Addie listened closely and made a mental note of who was complaining. Addie got up then and took her empty pot back home. She put all the details in her journal. *Would anything come of this argument? How involved were Ben, Harry and Reuben? Or were they saying things they didn't really mean just because they were challenged? Men were that way.*

Addie hadn't seen Tony there last night. He probably was the tattler that reported everything to Mr. Hardy. Sam always said Tony skulked around, that he never really did his work. He listened and got people in trouble.

Was Mr. Hardy a bad man? Did he cause accidents to happen, like Harry said? If that was true, Harry might be next. I need to watch him, but I can't get into the mill. I'd lose my anonymity in a minute. I'll have to get someone to watch at the mill.

Addie thought about it that night as she lay in bed before sleep came.

I guess this is one way I can use my sound mind, but I have no idea how to get someone to help me.

The next day, Addie's shoes were heavy logs on her feet. She trudged toward Seaside Place to get a good cup of coffee.

"Are you sick, Addie?" Ella Rose looked up and then again more closely.

"I'm in need of strong coffee, Ella Rose, and some good advice."

"How about a piece of apple pie, too? That cures a lot of problems."

"No, thanks." Addie found a chair at a vacant table. The place was nearly empty since it was still first shift.

Ella brought the coffee to Addie. "What's the problem, dear?"

"Oh, it's complicated."

"How can I help?"

"Just serve me more of that good coffee." Addie swallowed her desire to confide in her friend. Ella Rose smiled and filled her cup.

"To help you think."

Addie smiled and continued with her thought process.

Who can I ask? I don't know the mill workers. But Sam did! Let's see, he talked about Tony, that he was a bully. Sam thought he was Hardy's 'persuader.'

Who else? Someone with a low profile, a new worker or—I know! An outsider. He talked about Eddie George and some Chinese man. What was his name? Anyway,

Sam said Eddie lived across the way in the S'Klallam village called Little Boston. An outsider might just be the answer, if he would be willing.

What's in it for him? I suppose the Indians don't trust white people. After all, the mill owners made them move from their settlement here to across the bay for just the lumber to build new houses.

But I have to try. He's my best choice right now.

Ella Rose came by and picked up the empty cup and bustled back to the counter to help a new customer. The boards creaked as she passed by.

Addie worked at the general store with her father that afternoon. In between the sporadic sales and chats with customers, she hatched a plan that just might work. She determined to put it into action at the end of the first shift. The stop whistle blew before she knew it: Five-thirty.

"Father, I'll be a few minutes late getting home. I have an errand to do."

"Don't keep your mother waiting too long, Addie." He waved as Addie grabbed her shawl and sped out the door.

Addie walked quickly down to the bay and waited under a tree. A few cold drips went down her neck. Her hands quivered. *I hope I'm not too late. What would he say?*

She waited a few minutes until she saw him approaching.

A short Indian, barely five feet tall, walked toward the dock. Each silent step brought him closer to a cedar canoe moored there. Addie could tell it was perfect. Each chip by hand-held tools had hewn the hull into a smooth shell both in and out. It must be satisfying to own such a thing of beauty.

As he got nearer, she smelled him. The stench of sweat and dirty work clothes made her gasp and hold her nose. But it was no different than some of the men who ventured into the general store after working a shift. Soon the S'Klallam man would step into the sturdy vessel and paddle across Gamble Bay to his home and family. He didn't notice Addie until she stepped forward from under the trees.

"May I speak with you?" Her voice sounded hesitant.

"I am Eddie George. You may speak."

"My name is Addie Reagan. I am the widow of Sam Reagan, who worked in the mill. He had an accident and was killed last year."

"I remember him. A good man." Eddie nodded. "There is sadness in your eyes."

"Now, I must work because I have no husband. I chose to become a detective for Pinkerton's Agency."

"Peen-ker-tone? What's that?"

"They look for people breaking the law and see they are punished."

"Maybe there are some people breaking the law in Port Gamble. Is it not so?"

"I believe that's true, but I need help to find these people. Would you help me?"

"You want my help?"

"You work in the mill, don't you? I need someone—you—to watch and listen for these men who do wrong things. Because I am a woman, I would be too noticeable."

"And if I hear or see such things—?"

"Tell me."

Eddie's countenance changed to a totem face, and he thought for a while.

"I don't want to lose my job. There are bad things happening in the mill."

"We can meet here once a week maybe and you can tell me what you see and hear that week. Is that all right? I could give you a little money for the information."

"No money, but I will think about it." Eddie nodded and got into his canoe. He pushed off and dipped his paddle into the glassy water. He was gone.

Addie watched the wiry Indian recede into the distance, each movement fluid and purposeful.

I wonder. Will Eddie help me?

Chapter 17

The next morning, Addie walked to the general store, head down, so she didn't see him at first.

"Hey, lady, lady. We talk now, okay?" The small Chinese boy peeked from behind the big maple tree.

"You didn't come to my house." Addie joined him under the bare branches.

"I had work for Mrs. Smith."

"What's your name?"

"Chen Liu. Chen is family name."

"So, your particular name is Liu. Nice to meet you. I'm Addie." Addie held out her hand to shake, but Liu simply bowed. "Do you go to school here in Port Gamble?"

"No school for Chinese. You get trouble talking to me, too."

"I'm sorry to hear that. What do you want to learn?"

"Everything. English, history, math. No teacher for Chinese boy."

"I could do it," Addie said. "But I'll have to find a place where nobody will bother us first."

"Where?"

"I have an idea. Come here tomorrow at this time and we'll start lessons, okay?"

"I will try." Liu nodded several times and waved a small goodbye.

Addie worked a few hours at the general store. She ate her lunch of biscuits with slabs of last night's meat in the backroom, and then headed toward Seaside Place. The bells hooked on the knob jingled as she entered.

"Hello, friend," said Ella Rose.

"Ahh." Smells of cinnamon and yeast reached Addie's nose. "Cinnamon swirl bread again?" she asked.

Ella Rose smiled and handed her a thick slice with butter oozing over its surface. Addie took the plate and spent the next few minutes unrolling and eating the warm offering. An old man sat in the far corner.

"Ella Rose, could you help me?"

"I'd love to, dear. What are you concerned about?"

"I've met a little Chinese boy and he told me there's no school for him."

"So, you want to teach him?"

"Yes, and I need a quiet place to do that. I was thinking your storeroom, maybe?"

"Oh. I see. Yes, that could work. I'd have to move some bags of flour and set up a small table. I have stools."

"Could we start tomorrow? I'll help arrange the space."

"So quick! All right. I have a few minutes now, but I have to wait on customers, too." She looked around. "You all right, Frank?" The old man looked up.

"I could use another cup of coffee, Ella Rose." He held up the cup. His hair fell long and stringy over graying chin whiskers.

"I'll get the coffee pot, Ella Rose." Addie jumped up and brought the big blue pot to the man's table. "Here you are, sir."

"Thank you kindly, young lady." He took a sip and looked at her with lake blue eyes. "I've been listening to you talk with Ella Rose. That's a fine thing you're doing."

"You mean teaching the Chinese boy? I haven't started yet."

"But your intentions are good. And it seems to me you're determined to carry it through. Determination is big. Grit, yes, sir. That's what counts in this world."

"Why, thank you," said Addie. "I don't believe I know you. Are you new in town? My name is Addie May Murray Reagan."

"A long name for a small girl. My name's Frank Hall. I've been living here in Port Gamble for a few years. Live in a little cabin just outside the town limits. It's near the gambling joint. You know, Lucky Ace." The man put down his cup and ran a calloused hand across a face of tanned leather. Addie shook her head

"I thought I knew everything and everyone in town, since I've lived here all my nineteen years. Tell me about yourself."

"Not much to tell. I came here about five years ago. I lay low, try not to get into trouble and only come to Seaside Place once a month or so. Can't live too long without Ella Rose's cakes and pies." He looked toward Ella Rose. Was that a wink?

"You must have come in the general store some, but I don't remember seeing you before."

"Guess you weren't noticing." Frank took the toothpick he was sucking out of his mouth.

"Come on, Addie, we need to get this schoolhouse set up." Ella Rose called from the backroom door.

"Coming." Addie got up, grabbed the enameled coffee pot and returned it to the stove. Frank Hall straightened himself out like a carpenter unfolding a jointed ruler and shuffled out the door.

Ella Rose and Addie got busy shoving fifty-pound sacks of flour into one corner, stacking smaller sacks of sugar on the counter and sweeping a third corner where they set a small square table and two small stools from the café.

"I need to get the flour and sugar into bins soon, before the mice get to them." Ella Rosa set one fist on each hip and blew a strand of hair off her forehead.

"All set," said Addie. "And thanks ever so much, Ella Rose. I'll be back tomorrow about this time with Liu."

"Just be quiet about what you're doing, Addie. Not everyone likes the Chinese. I can't afford to lose customers."

"I'll be careful as a cat licking its paws." Addie squeezed her friend's arm and spun out the back door. She stopped back at the general store to buy two pencils and a tablet of paper. She put fifteen cents in the till and slipped out before her father saw her. He was occupied with waiting on Mrs. Murphy.

The next day, Addie waited for Liu by the big maple tree. A biting wind rattled the branches of the spreading tree and blew through her shawl to her skin. Liu pulled at her shawl and looked up with big eyes and a budding smile.

"I'm here, Miss Addie."

"Good, let's go where it's warm. I'll show you our little schoolroom." Addie tapped his back lightly and led the way to the back door of the café and bakery. Liu's eyes grew large as he sat down on the stool and picked up a newly sharpened pencil. He straightened the thin notebook Addie had bought him and sat up, waiting.

"Always come in the back door with me, Liu. Some people don't want to see people like you anywhere near them. I'm sorry that's true, but it is." Addie looked long at his half-moon eyes and his sealed lips.

"I know that is true." Liu dropped his head. "Thank you. You teach now, Miss Addie. I be good student." He picked up the pencil.

"Let's begin, then. Are you ready, Liu?" He nodded.

The time flew by. Liu listened to everything and then answered every question. Addie hated to stop, but the sun was heading like an old mare toward its stall. She gathered up the notebook and pencils. Liu put on his broadcloth jacket and a knitted cap. He promised to meet Addie again tomorrow.

The time was getting late. Addie grabbed her shawl and wrapped it tightly around her. She dashed out the door just as the mill whistle sounded through the low-hanging clouds. The call of an eagle raked through the forest, its screech lonely and unearthly.

Addie shivered and ran home.

Chapter 18

"I hear something this week." Eddie looked up from his squatting position.

"Yes?" Addie sat down on a rock and waited.

"Mr. Smith and Mr. Hardy talking. About milling timber from bracket claim. Must do it quickly."

"Bracket claim? What's that?"

"That's all I know. Couldn't hear the other words."

"Why would they need to do it quickly? The milling is always done quickly."

"Not so. Sometimes on second shift, a big raft of logs comes in. Must be done now, says Mr. Hardy. Everyone works very fast."

"Why is that?"

"It means logs were stolen from someone."

"How?"

"Maybe take some land in hidden place and cut down trees that not belong to Puget Mill."

"Oh! I hadn't thought of that," said Addie. "I must find out what or where this bracket is. Is it a place? Is it a claim?"

"Maybe bosses steal, but they're not killers. I don't know."

"Eddie, you did right to tell me. Thank you and keep listening." Addie watched him push off his canoe, swing his knees into the center of the boat's hull and tuck his toes under before dipping the paddle in the still waters of Gamble Bay. The S'Klallams who once lived on Port Gamble land now came over each morning from Point Julia.

Addie turned away and dashed toward home.

Tonight was the February social at the community hall. She needed to get ready. Addie washed her face and hands in the china bowl upstairs, after carrying a jug of hot water to her room. She spent extra time brushing and re-braiding her hair. She took out of her string purse the new blue ribbons she bought at the store today. After working them into her hair, she coiled braids on top of her head. No new dress, but that would change. Now she had money to save.

Addie arrived downstairs just as Mother took the ham out of the oven. It smelled of thyme and garlic.

"Bring the mashed potatoes, Addie, while I set this on the table. Get the gravy!"

Father tucked a cloth napkin into his collar, while Addie gathered up the potatoes and gravy. Mother swooped into the kitchen to bring the canned peaches and pickles.

"Another fine meal, Caroline," said Cameron

Murray, as he pushed back from his place at the end of the oak table.

"Thank you, dear," said Mother. "Now, Addie, the dishes."

Addie gasped. "I want to get to the social hall soon."

"Nevertheless, it is your duty to clean up after meals." Mother stood up and brought the platter laden with meat scraps to the sink counter.

Addie sighed and jumped up, gathering the dirty dishes into a pile. She bumped into her mother who was heading to the parlor. Plates shattered and bits of mashed potato splattered onto her skirt.

"Oh, no! I'll never get there now." Addie ran for the broom and dustpan and scraped up the debris from the floor. "I'll have to clean the floor now, too."

"Haste makes waste," Mother clucked her tongue and kept going to her easy chair. Father had already disappeared. Her mother always rested after dinner. This job was totally hers to finish.

Addie washed the dishes, scrubbed the floor and disposed of the garbage in record time. She dabbed at the bit of mashed potatoes stuck to her skirt. The last thing she did was use the lavender soap to wash her dishpan hands. "I hope the wrinkles disappear before I see Marcus," she said to herself.

Addie grabbed her deceased husband's

heavy coat and buttoned it as she walked to the community hall. Her parents weren't coming tonight for the valentine-themed evening. Marcus said he'd be there. Would he sit by her again?

The drizzly mist drifted down on Addie's head as she walked to the community hall. The wide porch had several steps and at the main door two gas lamp sconces burned brightly. Addie stepped into the room. A wave of heat hit her face She shrugged out her heavy coat and hung it in the coatroom. A buzz of young and older voices filled the auditorium. The schoolteacher, Miss Laura Benson, shepherded her schoolchildren to the first two rows of folding chairs.

Addie found some empty seats on the left side. She took one and immediately someone slipped into the other. A faint odor of pine and carbolic soap filled her nostrils.

"May I sit with you, Addie?"

"Oh, Marcus, of course. I thought I might see you here." Addie's cheeks felt warm when she smiled at her friend. "I think this is a night of recitations."

"Here's a program." Marcus held out a half sheet of paper. "First, it's 'The Gettysburg Address' by the schoolchildren."

"Did you ever memorize that in school?" asked Addie.

"Not until fifth grade or so. What about you?"

"Yes, I liked memorizing things." Just then,

Miss Benson introduced the first act. The children spoke quickly, and Addie mouthed the words along with them. They all returned to their seats murmuring their relief to each other.

Marcus moved a little closer to Addie, till his wool jacket rubbed against Addie's arm. The next act was a surprise: Cochran Smith got up on the stage and recited "Paul Revere's Ride" by Henry Wadsworth Longfellow. People in the audience leaned forward. It was an absorbing poem and so popular. Cochran spoke with feeling, but his hands fidgeted by his sides. Everyone applauded as he finished.

Finally, Sarah Larson stepped to the stage.

"I thought I'd recite the Love Chapter, First Corinthians 13, tonight, since in February we celebrate Valentine's Day, as well as some Presidents' birthdays. I hope you enjoy it."

She began: "If I speak with the tongue of men and of angels but have not love—" Marcus reached out and caught Addie's hand. Someone tapped Marcus on the shoulder. Addie jumped and jerked back her hand. She turned and saw Marianne looking down her nose at them. Marcus ignored Marianne and caught Addie's hand again. This time Addie shook her head and whispered "no." Addie raised her eyebrows at Marianne and turned back to the front.

After Sarah finished the familiar passage, Miss Benson said:

"The boys and girls are excited to make valentines. We'd like to invite everyone to make at least one tonight. We've set up some red, pink and white paper and some paper doilies, glue and scissors. If we could get some help re-arranging the room, we encourage you to create something for a special someone in your life."

The audience stood up as one and moved tables around the room to create workstations. The men passed folded chairs from hand to hand and put them on racks in the coatroom. Addie found a place at one table and grabbed a scissors. She folded a piece of red paper and cut a perfect arc that tapered to a point at the other end. She looked up for Marcus, but she couldn't spot him. While she was busy gluing and composing a little poem, a pair of strong hands pressed a valentine in her hand and vanished. She stepped away from the table to read it, retreating to the coatroom.

"I'm glad we're friends," it said. "Could we be something more?" Addie sucked in her breath. On the back side, it was signed "MW." Addie stretched her neck like a heron and looked all around the room. She saw Marcus in a corner, gazing at her. She held up the Valentine and smiled at him, nodding her head. He grinned and moved through the clusters of people toward her.

But, before he got to her, a horn blared outside. Three long blasts—There was an accident at the mill! Addie's mind flashed back to that terrible moment when she first heard Sam was killed. She sat down, unable to hold back the waves of grief that rolled over her. She sobbed quietly, but her whole body convulsed.

Has another life been cut short? I can't bear it!

CHAPTER 19

Addie recovered her composure after a few moments. After she wiped her face with a handkerchief, she ran toward the nearest door. She didn't see Marcus. He must have run out another door. Meanwhile, people in the hall cleared out like fleas off a drowning rat.

It was futile to go to the mill. Whoever was injured would be brought on a stretcher to the little hospital in Port Gamble. Addie ran to the doorstep. Just two rooms squeezed into a small saltbox cabin, but it was well equipped. Marcus came up behind her and joined her by the door. Addie peered in.

Lydia Reed, the nurse, propelled herself into action, putting new sheets on the examining table and setting out clean instruments. She went to a medicine cupboard and then drew out a bottle of something and rolls of gauze bandages. Lines grooved her face. People from the social hall streamed into the hospital courtyard.

A commotion drifted up the road from the sawmills. Men shouted at each other. The two policemen at Port Gamble directed the gruesome procession. Two men carried a man's body on a canvas stretcher. It was covered by someone's coat, but one arm hung over the side. Everyone involved was saturated in blood. All the men who followed showed the impact of the event in their stony faces and eyes deep as wells with the memory.

"Clear a path," shouted the two officers, and put their arms out to shield the stretcher and its occupant. Curiosity put the crowd on tiptoes to see who it was, knowing the same could happen to them.

"It's Harry," shouted someone. "Harry Jensen."

Whispers swirled through the group. Addie gasped. She turned to Marcus.

"I went to a gathering of old friends two weeks ago. Harry was complaining loudly about working conditions," she whispered into Marcus' ear. "Is that just a coincidence?"

Marcus shrugged his shoulders. "Hard to say."

The men brought Harry into the hospital. Lydia immediately closed the door and bolted it with a loud click. The group stepped back. Some drifted away, but many stayed to hear what would happen. Marcus found a spot on a log bench and motioned for Addie to sit next to him.

"You're shivering, Addie." He put his coat around her.

"It's the shock, not the drizzle," said Addie. Marcus creased his eyebrows.

The log bench sat under a cedar tree, its

shaggy branches a green umbrella against the drizzle. They heard moans and then shrieks, as treatment must have progressed. As time dragged on, Addie remembered her coat left at the social hall. Marcus went to retrieve it. When he returned, John Deming, assuming his duties as part-time physician in Dr. Spencer's absence, emerged through the door followed by Nurse Reed. Their blood-smeared clothing and spattered faces told a story that needed no words.

"Dear people," said Deming, "We tried our best, but Harry's injuries were too serious and extensive. I'm afraid we lost him." He hung his head, turned and went back into the hospital. Lydia Reed pulled the door closed as she disappeared, also.

Gasps then silence filled the heavy mist. The clusters of people, like the spent clouds, drifted away. Marcus supported Addie's arm and walked her home.

Once home and in her room, Addie wrote in her notebook about all that had happened recently. There were a lot of events to make sense of. Addie sat on the bed.

What do I know so far? This latest accident can't be a coincidence. Harry complained loudly at the gathering less than two weeks ago, and now he's dead. Tony was there and he's known to be an enforcer for Hardy. But, did Hardy tell him to spy on everyone who attended that party? And does he hang around other events so he can report who the troublemakers are to—To whom? Jake Hardy for one.

What about Mr. Smith? Is he the moving force to identify and suppress unrest at the mill? He seems to be ambitious, hard. Is he hiding anything? I wouldn't be surprised if he was involved in something shady. How can I find out more about him? I must ask Eddie or maybe Marcus. But I can't reveal why I want to know. Could Marcus be involved, too? I hate to think that, but I do remember he said he needed money urgently.

Or does the involvement go all the way up to Mr. Ames? There's no evidence of that so far. Liu seems to know something, though. I wonder what it is. I'll have to ask him where he works. Does he have parents here in Port Gamble? Is he an orphan? I sure hope not.

Addie rolled onto her stomach and wrote a few more notes in her notebook.

Eddie said he saw Hardy and Smith talking together recently. I wonder what they discussed besides the illegal cutting of timber. I must find out what or where bracket is. And, did someone direct Tony to shove Harry into the saw blades? Did he act alone for another reason? Or was it someone else?

There are so many unanswered questions. Where do I start? I need to find out if Jake and Smith are as guilty as they seem. That won't be easy. I wonder if there is another person—an outsider—who could listen on night shift.

Addie made a list: *First, find someone on second shift that will be a listener for me. Two, find out what bracket means. Three: find out if someone pushed Harry into the saws.* She sat up, shut her notebook and put it on her side table.

Well, I have a plan, but how do I find out the information I need? And who will help me on second shift?

I have one more thing to write in my notebook. Four: decide if I like Marcus. And trust him. He seems so nice and my sad heart wants to believe him. But I think he's holding back something, and I don't know what it is yet. Addie sighed. She uncoiled her hair and let the ribbons fall onto the bed. She put them on the table, and then brushed her flowing hair.

Pastor Deming told us once the verse about using our sound minds. I sure hope I'm thinking straight. If I find out someone is doing wrong here at the mill, I might put myself in a dangerous position. If only I could be a real investigator! But, if I report labor agitators, maybe they'll get killed. I don't want that. I'm all for law and order, but not treachery and murder.

Will I ever find a love like Sam's again in my life? That was surely a one-time thing. He loved me for myself. He liked the things I liked. Now, I'm back with my mother who doesn't like anything I do, all because she couldn't have another child after me.

It's all too soon. Too much. I'm not ready.

Addie lay down with a heavy heart.

Chapter 20

It was Monday afternoon and Addie was worried. Liu was late for his school lessons. Addie tramped into Seaside Place's kitchen and admired some of the molasses cookies Ella Rose had just taken out of the oven.

"Now, keep your hands off, Addie. Well, maybe one cookie," Ella conceded. Addie grabbed one before her friend could change her mind. Just then, she heard a scratching at the back door. She swirled around and sprinted toward it.

"Miss Addie, I bring my mother." Liu gestured to a small woman with tiny feet. She bowed low.

"Hello, Miss Addie. I am Chen Jiao." She bowed again.

"Come in, please, Mrs. Chen." Addie bowed and then ushered her in.

"Thank you for teaching Liu, my son. He smart boy. Needs to learn."

"I agree. I do my best."

"I am here because my boss, Mrs. Martha Smith, is away now. She went to San Francisco to buy new clothes for her family."

"Would you like to listen to the lesson, too? Can you stay?"

"I like that. I need lessons in English, too. My husband is very smart. He is a philosopher and professor. At least, he was so in Shanghai."

"Is that where you came from? Now, what does he do?"

"He works at the mill, doing heavy work. It tears at his soft hands."

"Why did you come? That doesn't seem like a good job for him."

"It's not. But we had no choice. We were all working in the garden in front of our house. Two men came by. They were American sailors. They asked, 'Do you want a job in America?' He said no, but the men grabbed both his arms and dragged him to a covered cart. Then, they grabbed Liu and me, too. We landed on a boat in the harbor. They left the harbor chop-chop and sailed toward the rising sun. Many days later we came to San Francisco and then on to this cold and rainy place."

"I'm so sorry. They forced you to come here. But now, what do you do here?"

"I work in Mrs. Smith's house. I'm the cook, and Liu, he spends much time in the basement ironing shirts, sheets and fancy dresses."

"I hope they pay you. Will you go back some day to China?"

"They pay, but they think Chinese don't need so much money. We are barbarians, Mrs. Smith says." Mrs. Chen tightened both fists. "We are not barbarians. We come from an ancient and respected culture. We have education in our country. We are from the highest class in our society."

"It must be difficult for you."

"You are a sympathetic lady. I would like to give you a gift for teaching Liu. What can I do?"

"I don't need payment, but could I ask you to do something for me?

"Yes. What is it?"

"Could you listen to conversations in the Smith house? I mean talk about what's happening in this town. I think some bad things are happening to workers and I want to report it to the police."

"You are brave, Mrs. Addie. For you, My English is not good, but I listen. When I have something, I send a message with Liu. And, I will make you my special dumplings."

"Thank you! You will be a great help to me."

"I do hear things, but I don't know what they mean."

"When you hear something, just tell me what you hear, even if it's just a few words. Sometimes the smallest detail can be important."

Mrs. Chen was listening with eyes on Addie. She nodded.

Addie tried something new. "Have you ever heard Mr. or Mrs. Smith mention 'bracket'?"

"No." Mrs. Chen shook her head. She stopped

and thought a minute. "I heard something, but I don't think it means anything."

"What was it? Everything is important to me." Addie leaned toward the small Chinese woman.

"Mrs. Smith said something about a bracket claim. Mr. Smith was worried about the trees there. Does that mean anything to you?"

"A bracket claim? That could be important. Thank you." Addie reached out to touch the woman's arm, but she bowed several times and said "*Xièxiè*. (shay-shay)."

Mrs. Chen bowed. "Now I must go back to their house and make food for dinner." She turned her slender body and trotted toward executive row.

"My father hears things in the mill," said Liu, as they sat down again to study.

"I would like to meet your father. I want to ask him a question."

"I will talk to him soon. You are good person, Miss Addie. He help you."

Addie smiled. She and Liu worked on understanding compound nouns.

"Why does 'schoolhouse' mean something different than 'house school?'" said Liu. He scratched his nose.

"The order of the words in English is important and can change the meaning if re-arranged," said Addie. "So, 'horse cart' means something different than 'cart horse'." She laughed. "It's confusing, isn't it?"

Liu's head bobbed up and down.

"That's enough for today." Addie closed the reader she had used as a child. She and Liu made arrangements to meet again in a couple of days. Long after Liu left, Addie sat at the improvised desk in the back of Ella Rose's bakery.

What was a bracket claim? Who should I ask? Is it connected to any criminal activity? I need to follow my instructions and find what's happening at the mill—the labor agitation. Concentrate, Addie!

Addie jotted notes on a piece of paper. She slipped it into her small beaded bag and strolled to Seaside Place. She ordered a cup of coffee.

"Addie." A familiar male voice called out.

"Marcus." She moved toward his table. "I didn't expect to see you here." He stood and helped seat her. The chair balked as it slid over the sawdust on the floor.

"I have a few hours off. I've been sharpening the saws for hours."

"Oh, that's why the mills have been quieter than usual."

"Yes. Say, I see you're not working your regular hours at the general store. Is everything all right with you?" Marcus' eyebrows arched over those glacier blue eyes. Addie had to look away or be distracted.

"Hm?"

"Are you all right? Everything okay at home?" He reached for her arm.

"I'm fine--just a bit busy." She shrank back. "What do you do with your free time?"

"There's a place down the road I frequent. I like to play cards."

"At Lucky Ace?" Marcus' eyebrows shot up.

"Sometimes. Not too much. How do you know about that place?"

"Someone mentioned it to me." Addie paused. "In my spare time, I give school lessons to a little Chinese boy."

"Is that wise? The Chinese are kept separate from everyone else."

"Do you disapprove?"

"No. It's just that you might get comments and snubs if you associate with them."

"After losing my baby, I see things differently. I don't care much what people think. Liu is a nice boy, and eager to learn. He needs a chance in life." She watched Marcus, her face a mask. He was silent for a moment, just staring at Addie.

"I had no idea."

"Did I tell you I was married?"

"No."

"Well, now I'm widowed and not a mother, either." Addie's chin quivered. "You may as well know."

"Why do you teach the Chinese boy?" Marcus moved on to another subject as his ears turned scarlet. "Do you need the extra money?"

"I do it for free," said Addie in a louder voice.

"You've been through a lot, Addie, and yet you want to help someone in need? You're a saint. I know if I were doing it, I would ask for payment."

"Don't you make a good salary, Marcus?"

"Sure, but it never hurts to have extra money. You might need it for something you didn't expect to happen."

"I hope that's not your problem, Marcus."

"Don't you worry about me, Addie. I have resources you know nothing about."

"That sounds mysterious." She fluttered her eyelashes.

Did I just do that?

"And, by the way, Addie. I do think you care about what people think. Or at least, what I think." Marcus took her hand and kissed it. Addie just looked at him. She couldn't breathe. He leaned forward.

The clock on the wall bonged four times.

"I must fly," said Addie, jumping up. "Goodbye, Marcus. It was fun talking with you." She raced toward the door.

"Can we sit together at the horn recital?" He called after her.

"Perhaps. See you then." Addie waved as she walked out the door.

What is Marcus after? Whatever it is, I'm not ready!

Addie avoided seeing Marcus around the town the next few days. If she saw him sitting at a table at Seaside Place, she pivoted around and out the door. If he sauntered down one of the paths at the town center, Addie dashed behind a bush or into a door—any door. She once dashed into the barbershop. Several shaggy faces peered out from behind newspapers and snapped them to express their sense of outrage for the invasion. Anyway, it seemed that way.

Why did I burst out about my miscarriage? That's private and painfully personal. Guess I'm still hurting. Guess I'm still an emotional woman. I wouldn't blame Marcus if he dropped our friendship.

I really don't care so much about what people think. This is what I am. This is what I've lost. I want people to know I was with child. I was going to have Sam's baby. I was going to be a mother. Now, I have nothing. What's my future? Will I be remembered for anything when I die? Will I be just a sad spinster the rest of my life??

If I can make good and become a Pinkerton's agent, maybe I can do some good. That's the one thing I'm clinging to for now.

Addie walked and walked along the seashore. It was an extremely low tide. Her shoes caught repeatedly on the clusters of oysters that bristled from all the large rocks. Little crabs skittered sideways from under shadowed places. Pools of saltwater shimmered from a dozen different indentations in the rocks. The sun came out from behind a gray cloud and sparkled on the surf-polished rocks. Addie sighed.

Teekalet really was a good name for this place. 'Brightness of the noonday sun.' Seeing the beauties of this part of the world gives me peace and maybe a bit of hope. Nature seems to restore me.

Addie picked up her skirts so she wouldn't get them wet. She tiptoed back to the lawn and the path back to the general store.

Time to get back to work.

CHAPTER 21

Addie heard them before she reached the community hall door. A throaty French horn soared over the deep belches of the tubas and blats of trombones and trumpets. She chuckled. The dissonance of sound as they warmed up would smooth into a blend of liquid tones as the performance started. But it would be loud.

Addie found a seat about two-thirds back in the auditorium. She was early this time, so she had her choice of seats. She saved one on the end, just in case. People streamed in two or three at a time. Soon, Marcus slipped in the seat on the end next to her.

"Hello," he said. "Who's playing tonight?"

"Do you know George Frederick? He's playing the tuba. Some of the mill workers are playing a trumpet trio, too. Here's a program I picked up in the back."

Addie handed him the list of songs and players.

"Are they good? Some of these selections are difficult."

"Oh, yes. There are always some good musicians

that come to Port Gamble. I think Mr. Pope and Mr. Talbot encourage that."

"Oh, really? Mill workers? That's unusual."

"They wanted to promote wholesome activities in this isolated community, Their New England religious upbringing, I'm told," said Addie. "There's a great baseball team here, too. Just wait until summer."

"Fascinating. It hardly seems like there's time for entertainment with the long days everyone works."

"Well, music's a better choice than drinking and gambling, according to the big bosses. I do agree."

"Ladies and gentlemen—"

"It's starting!" Addie sat up straighter in the folding chair. Marcus reached and touched her hand. Addie felt the warmth of his palm. She smiled at him.

The group of horns started with a Sousa march. The people in the front rows covered their ears, but others tapped their toes. Several marches later, they switched to classical—a Haydn number. Next, a French horn solo that made Addie think of a foxhunt with horns echoing in the woods.

"I love the French horn," Addie whispered to Marcus' ear. Something hit her cheek—a pebble! She picked it up from her lap and rubbed the sting from her cheek. She looked around and saw someone staring at her from the back row. Tony

Esposito's face sported a closed mouth smile with eyebrows raised high. He cocked his head to the side and covered his mouth in pretended apology. Addie narrowed her eyes and looked away.

"What's wrong?" Marcus glanced around.

"Just a prankster," said Addie. "Nothing to worry about."

The concert finished and everyone headed to the refreshment table. Addie watched as people loaded up plates with apple pie, ginger cake, scones and molasses cookies.

"I can see why these events are popular," said Marcus.

"Lots of lonely men far away from home?" said Addie.

"No, lots of desserts to encourage everyone's sweet tooth." He laughed.

"It sure brightens a dull winter evening," said Addie. She walked toward a table with a plate of apple pie. Suddenly, she stumbled. The plate flew out of her hand and landed on the floor with her. Addie felt pie on her cheek.

"Excuse me," someone said with exaggerated inflection. "Let me help you." A large hand reached down. Addie went for it, and then saw who offered it.

"Tony Esposito, why are you bothering me?" Addie composed herself then pushed herself off the floor and to a standing position. She brushed by Tony, who was laughing.

"Kind of clumsy, aren't you? Maybe you should take care of your own business and not bother the mill workers."

"What are you talking about?" Addie's eyes locked onto Tony's.

"I see everything," he said, and walked away.

Marcus, who had gone to get help with cleanup, came forward.

"I wouldn't want Tony targeting me, if I were you. What was he talking about?"

"I don't know," Addie said. "I've done nothing to bother him." She wiped some crumbs off her dress. Marcus took a handkerchief from his pocket and brushed a smear of apple off her cheek.

"All right. Do you want to try again with dessert?"

"No, I just want to go home."

"I think I'd better walk you there. Let's get our coats." They walked to the coatroom and took their damp jackets off the hooks.

Marcus took her hand as they strolled along.

"You're trembling, Addie," he said, giving her hand a kiss.

"That incident upset me, Marcus."

"You've been preoccupied this week. Your thoughts are somewhere else most of the time."

"It reminded me of my husband's accident," said Addie.

"No, no, but tell me what's changed. Can you do that?"

"I have a new project. I can't say much more than that."

"Oh, interesting! Tell me more."

"I really can't."

"Does it involve Mr. Smith? I overheard him talking last night to a lumber buyer in his office."

"Were you spying on him?"

"He has a booming voice, Addie."

"Go on."

"Well, he was concerned about some purchase of land for logging."

"Is that all you heard? How many logs would it be?"

"That I didn't hear—but a lot of acres of trees. It always is."

Addie stopped to listen to the night air. She should have heard only quiet forest sounds, but this was Port Gamble. Instead, the saws screeched and droned on.

"Were they doing something illegal? Why were they speaking in hushed tones?"

Marcus shrugged his shoulders. "It's better not to talk too loudly about this," he said. "It seems the forest has ears, even though the saws drown out the peace."

He kissed her hand. "You seem awfully interested."

Addie withdrew her hand. "Just normal curiosity." She looked away from him. "Here we are at my house."

"I enjoyed our time together tonight. Let's continue to enjoy each other's company, okay?"

"I, too, had a good time. You're a good friend." She smiled at him and ran up the few steps to the back porch. "Goodnight."

"Goodnight, Addie." Marcus shoved his bare hands into his pockets. "I hope you've thought about my valentine a couple of weeks ago. I do want us to be more than friends."

"I treasure that valentine, and I'm thinking on it." She smiled and gave a little wave. "Bye."

"Addie, Addie, give me an answer, do." He grinned and shuffled down the street into the mist.

"I'm home," Addie called out and went directly up to her room.

It seems I have a beau. Can I trust him? He's pushing too fast. I still get the feeling he's hiding something. Why does he live with the Smiths? Is Mr. Smith grooming him for a management position? Is he spying on the mill workers? He goes there often enough to sharpen the saws. I want to like him. But, what do I know of him? And why did he tell me about the discussion he overheard? To see if I might have knowledge of what sounds like the Brackett claim timber rustling? Or was he part of that discussion? Is he trying to help me or entrap me?

Addie jotted a few notes in her journal of observations and went to bed. The rain dripped off the roof at the cracked gutter outside her window.

On Friday, Addie met Eddie George at the usual

place. This time, though, she was careful to keep herself hidden.

"Eddie, come over here behind these bushes." She beckoned to the short man. His face, the color of well-polished mahogany, registered no emotion. He padded toward her without a sound.

"Why do you hide?"

"Tony Esposito threatened me a few days ago. He says he sees everything. So, I wanted to warn you."

"He is a bad man. I'll be careful. You should, too. Maybe he didn't see you. Maybe he just thinks you are a threat to him."

"Maybe somebody else saw us and told him. Anyway, we both should be careful. If you don't want to continue, I would understand."

"I will help you. There is evil here in Port Gamble."

"What have you heard lately?"

"Mr. Smith stopped by the mill three days in a row. There were a lot of logs to cut into boards. He always talks to Jake Hardy when he comes. I got as near as I could to hear them. I heard Smith say, 'Sam Reagan was on to us.' What does that mean?"

"It means Sam understood what they were doing. Was it something illegal?"

"I think so, because Hardy also said, "That's why Reagan had an accident."

"He said that?" Addie's voice rose.

"Shh. Yes, he did. See, they are bad men."

"Thank you for telling me. Keep listening, but—be careful." Addie dismissed him and he stepped toward his boat. Eddie looked in all directions, then pushed off his canoe and jumped into the hull.

Addie walked through the underbrush until she reached the post office. She entered and composed a letter to Agent Jamison: her thirty-day report.

"Addie, is anything wrong?" said Sarah. She took Addie's letter and put a stamp on it. "A letter to Pinkerton's?"

"It's my thirty-day report. I'm one-third through my probationary period. Sixty days to go with no definite solution yet." Addie sighed.

"You have plenty of time. Keep looking." Sarah gave her a hug.

CHAPTER 22

Addie shuffled home, thoughts whirling. She ate dinner with her mother and father, but she couldn't remember a single bit of the conversation. She performed her usual dishwashing duties and plodded up to her room.

Addie fell on her bed and looked up at the ceiling. She remembered the first time she met Sam.

He was tall and built thin. But he could hook any log and roust it onto the conveyer belt for the saws. The story developed that Addie stubbed her toe on a rock while walking by him. But it really was Sam's wink that rattled her. Anyway, she stumbled toward him. He caught her and put his arms out to keep her from falling. She felt his hard arm muscles, and his gentle hands. She thanked him and apologized. He invited her to Seaside Place for coffee.

Sam talked and talked. Addie learned all about his childhood: he liked riding horses and grooming them. He hated snakes. He helped on his dad's farm and got strong throwing hay bales into wagons. His dad was named Samuel Adam Reagan and he was named Samuel Alan Reagan.

His mother was named Linnea: she was Swedish. That's where he got his blond hair. His dad had coffee-colored hair. His younger sister, who died after five days of fever, had auburn hair. His grandfather fought in the Civil War and passed his 1851 Navy revolver on to his son. Now, Sam had it.

When Sam stopped to take a deep breath and a gulp of coffee, Addie told a little about herself. Then they heard the end-of-day whistle. Ella Rose came by and collected their coffee cups.

"Doesn't your mother need you at home, Addie?"

"What? Oh, it's almost dinner time!" Addie did jump up at that point and said, "Maybe you'd like to come by sometime for dinner, Sam. Not tonight, of course, because my mother wants to know first if someone's been invited." She smiled.

"Thank you, I'd like that. When can we meet again, Addie?"

"I have some time tomorrow. When is your regular shift over?"

"Come to Seaside Place after your evening meal? Say seven-thirty?"

"I'll do my best. Thanks for the coffee." She waved and hurried out the door.

The conversation resumed the next evening and every day after that. After three weeks, Sam met her at the social hall. He sat beside her and stared at her profile, drawing her hair back with one callused finger.

"Can we talk afterward?" he whispered.

She nodded, a feeling like fluttering baby birds in her stomach. After the music ended, Sam grabbed her hand and led her out the back way. They disappeared into the misty darkness and headed for shelter under a giant spruce.

"Addie, I want to ask you something."

She gulped and nodded.

"Do you love me? I love you. I've known it since the day we met."

"I think I do, Sam. I love you, too."

"Could we get married? I want to live with you and be your husband and your best friend."

Addie let out a squeal. She composed herself and answered, "Yes. Oh, yes. I don't know what my parents will say, but I say yes."

Sam unbuttoned his flannel shirt pocket and took out a ring. He put it on Addie's finger.

"This ring was my mother's. Dad bought her a diamond ring for a huge sum: fifty dollars. I want you to wear it now."

"It's beautiful, Sam." Addie admired her hand. She hadn't picked at her fingernails since she met Sam. The ring sparkled and her nails looked glossy and even. Sam leaned forward and pressed his warm lips to hers. She felt a current flow through her.

They married a week later, though Addie's mother heartily disapproved.

"You're not eighteen yet, Addie."

"I will be in ten days. Will you make me wait until then? Sam and I love each other."

Her father intervened. "We hope you've thought this through. It's not just because you lust after each other, is it?

"No, Father." Addie blushed.

Her Father made the arrangements and paid for the preacher. They had a church wedding with a bouquet of foxgloves, ferns and yellow hollyhocks that came from their garden. Ella Rose made a vanilla cake with powdered sugar icing and piped yellow roses around the top. They cut the cake outside under a canvas awning, basking in a rare early July day of sunshine, full of blue sky and singing birds. The cracked glass cry of an eagle, the calling of red-breasted robins and the cooing of doves serenaded their guests. Addie wore her grandmother's wedding dress, a high-necked lace bodice with a sweep of white satin and full skirts. Addie wore a crown of yellow roses fashioned by Sarah Larson, who picked them herself early that morning.

"Addie, you have stars in your eyes," Sam whispered in her ear. "You're beautiful."

"Sam Reagan, you're nice to look at yourself, with that new silk vest and a real bow tie."

Sam laughed out loud and drew Addie toward him. They kissed a long, proper kiss, like they really were man and wife. Addie looked away.

"Should we let everyone see us acting this way, Sam?"

"I think it's allowed on our wedding day, dear wife." He kissed her again. She laughed and kissed him back.

After the wedding, Addie moved her few clothes and books to the married couples' quarters. Sam had rented it a few days earlier. He carried her through the door and set her down.

"Welcome to your new home, Mrs. Reagan."

Addie wrapped her arms around herself as she remembered Sam's gentle embraces. Sam took the next day off for their honeymoon. Each day they had together was filled with love, laughter and talk about the future.

Sam went back to work and Addie spent her days helping her father at the general store. An hour before quitting time, Addie took the short walk to the shared room where she'd see her Sam and bask in his love.

The room had a sink with a mirror and an indoor toilet down the hall, but it had no kitchen. They ate their meals in the dining hall just after the workers ate. The workers shoveled bowls of baked beans, mashed potatoes and meat into their ravenous mouths. A long day produced a raging hunger. The second seating included wives and, therefore, the men minded their manners.

Were all newly married people so absorbed with their love? Addie didn't know, but she suspected so. Sam and Addie clung to each other like drowning persons to a rescuer. And they talked about everything. It was just so fun to have hope and a future together.

One night, Sam told Addie:

"There's been some trouble at the mill."

"What kind of trouble?"

"Some of the men worry about getting hurt. We all know it's a dangerous job. That's one reason it pays well. If I can hold out for a few more months, maybe we could buy a small parcel of land near here."

"That would be wonderful. This is a nice room, but it would be so nice to have our own home. I could cook for you. We could have more privacy, too."

"That's what I promise to provide you, as soon as I can."

"What was the matter at the mill, then, if everybody agrees it's dangerous?"

"The management isn't so excited about making safety improvements. It will cost money to set up barriers and guards for fingers and such. Some of the men got angry and started shouting."

"Did you shout?"

"Sure, Addie. We have to stand up for our rights. Personally, I'm in favor of forming a union. That's the way of the future."

"I'm sure that the big bosses wouldn't like that," said Addie. "They have their hand in every part of the mill's running. They wouldn't want to give up any control."

"You are right, Addie. Perceptive of you." Sam kissed her on the cheek.

"Be careful, Sam. We can't push the management around too much. That would be dangerous. You might lose your job."

"I'll be careful. I don't trust Jake Hardy and his associates. He's ambitious."

They kissed and went to sleep. Two days later, Sam fell into the saws and was killed. Paralyzed by grief, Addie couldn't hold a serious thought in her head. Now, more than twelve months after the death, she had begun to think it all through.

The facts didn't add up.

CHAPTER 23

Mr. Smith or Jake Hardy or both of them may have caused Sam's accident. How could anyone be so cruel? A little nudge, a slight bump on the back, an accidental trip—it could happen so easily and still look like an accident. And once the person fell forward, the saw's turning would draw someone relentlessly into the toothy monster.

Tears streaked down Addie's cheeks as she imagined Sam's alarm and then terror as his suspenders pulled him into a death trap.

How could I find proof that this actually happened? I only have an overheard conversation. It was hearsay. Eddie's testimony might not be admitted as evidence in a court of law. And the defense lawyer would try to discredit Eddie George, the most honest man I know, because of his ruddy skin.

Don't I have Sam's suspenders?

Her little pile of his belongings rested in her trunk. Addie sat up and swung her legs over the edge of the bed. With a scrape, she slid the trunk from under the bed. Would it be there? If it were there, it would certainly be ripped to shreds. Just like my Sam's body. Addie grabbed her stomach as a knot tightened deep inside. After rubbing her abdomen a while, she opened the trunk and searched for Sam's stuff. The events around the accident, blurred with shock and pain, remained sketchy in her mind. If only she could put down on paper her remembrance of that time.

Addie found the bundle wrapped with Sam's linen shirt. She found it hard to swallow down the tight lump that stuck in her throat. The suspenders weren't in the bundle. She rolled the contents back up. Running her hands down the sides of the trunk, she felt around the edges and under the folded pillowcases and tablecloths. Some she had never used in her three-month marriage to Sam.

Maybe the suspenders were so shredded they had been discarded. But if she couldn't find them, the story the workers told still might be true. Who was it that told her? She thought back to that time: the news, the sprint to the mill, the cluster of workers shielding her from the truth, the arm with Sam's flannel shirt still on it.

If she did find them and they were chewed to pieces, that would mean the story was true, but would not prove someone pushed Sam. Her hand finally touched something on the bottom of the trunk. She pulled it out, hoping—Hoping what? Addie opened her hand. She held Sam's red and yellow suspenders. But they had no marks on them whatsoever.

Addie collapsed onto the bed and curled into a ball, like a newborn.

Here was real evidence. But what did it prove? Sam

wasn't wearing his suspenders when he was drawn into the saws. Somebody was lying about that? Did they lie about the other details, too?

Maybe the workers wanted to shield her from the truth. Maybe Sam did get shoved. Or maybe he slipped on the fine sawdust always present on the floor of the mill. If what Eddie heard was true, either Jake Hardy or Elliot Smith could be a murderer. Accidents happened often in the mill. What about Harry's accident and death recently? Her mind raced on. So, this pattern of behavior has happened at least twice and maybe more. She doubled over in pain. She wanted to retch, to get the vile filth out of her body, out of her mind. Instead, she sat up and clenched her fists.

This must stop! I'll find the proof.

"Addie, go and get some vegetables from the root cellar." Mother's voice cut through the thick haze of Addie's thoughts. Addie rubbed the tears from her eyes and planted her feet on the floor. She took a moment to freshen her face with a splash of water and blotted it with a piece of towel. Addie ran to the stairs and took them two at a time. She reached the main floor before her mother could call again.

Why was she in the kitchen so late?

"Got it, Mother. Are squash, onions and carrots okay?" she said as she breezed by.

"Fine. Then come and pare the vegetables for the cook pot." Mother stopped her stirring. "I'm planning to make a bean soup for tomorrow. You know that means putting the whole thing on to simmer on the back burner tonight."

Addie continued out the door and to the small shed behind the house. A whizzing sound like a hummingbird's beating wings passed by her ear. She stopped and batted at the bird. But it wasn't a bird. Addie heard something hit the trunk of the apple tree nearby. She went over to touch it. It was sharp and shiny—a bullet! Addie ran for the shed and dove into the pile of potatoes. She stayed there for several minutes, but nothing else happened.

Is someone warning me off? Or was it a random bullet? I'll never know, but this I do know: Something evil is happening in Port Gamble and I must root it out.

Addie's trembling hands grabbed a small pumpkin, an onion, plus two long carrots and hurried back to the house to prepare the vegetables.

I have a sound mind. I know Sam loved me. Now, I need to find a way to turn in the complainers, and also find the evildoers. But, do I have the power?

"I'll turn the screws on those lazy slackers," said Jake Hardy. "They won't have time to agitate for safety or for unions." He slammed his fist on

Mr. Smith's mahogany desk. The paperweight jumped an inch.

"I'm glad you agree with me, Hardy," said Mr. Smith, pacing back and forth.

"Now go back and take care of it."

Hardy stalked out the door and set a course for the mill, feet pumping. He scratched his head and furrowed his eyebrows.

Did Mr. Smith mean he should talk to those men, maybe threaten them? Or did it mean something more? Mr. Smith never explained himself, but you could always count on him wanting more money, more profits.

Hardy set his jaw and looked around.

I'll see to it that any complainer gets his due. Whatever it takes.

He strode back to the mill and walked up and down the production line.

That Indian kept his eyes on his wide push broom.

"Keep that floor clean, George. We don't want sparks starting a fire." Jake slapped him on the back. Eddie George jumped, and then pushed faster. "Chen, keep shoving that board through the planer. And stack it up chop-chop." He laughed as his joke. Chen gave no response but a blank face.

"You really don't understand, do you?" said Hardy and moved down the line. He prodded the men who stacked wood, those who shoved the massive logs onto the conveyer belt, and the guy who kept a tally of board feet produced.

The whistle sounded and the men stepped away from the line. They gathered their jackets and hats and filed out the door. Within half an hour, the next shift stepped to their stations and started up the saws again. The shrieking sound of saws never stopped. The blizzard of sawdust never settled long. Jake Hardy shook the hand of the night foreman and breathed a sigh. He clapped his hat onto his head and got out of the mill at double speed.

"Whew. It couldn't come any faster. I was suffocating in there." Jake took a big gulp of cold pine-scented air and made for his home. His pace quickened. He'd soon see his wife Sophie and his two children, Andy and Amy. He stomped up the stairs and heard shrieks and giggles behind the door. He burst in and caught one child under each arm. He twirled them around a few times and set them down.

"Oh, Jake, we're so glad to see you." His wife Sophie limped from the kitchen to give him a kiss. "Supper will be ready in just a minute. Children, go wash your hands." Four small feet hit the floor and skidded across the pine floorboards to get to the hand-washing sink first.

Sophie brought a tureen of soup to the table, while the children finished dousing their hands and ran to sit at the kitchen table. Jake sat down hard in his chair and began unlacing his boots. He pulled off one and then the other. Amy pinched her nose and looked at Andy, who let out a snort.

"Yes, I know my feet are smelly, but I promise to wash after supper. I'm starving." He eyed the two children who sat up straight, while Sophie brought a plate of freshly baked bread and a pot of butter to the table.

"It smells and look delicious. Thanks to you, Sophie, for making our home an oasis from the relentless industry that consumes so much of my time."

"Let's eat, Daddy," said Amy. Jake grinned and took a big helping.

❧

"Oh, Mary, life is so crazy," said Addie, taking a gulp of coffee.

"What's happened?"

"I can't really tell you, that's the problem. Just a project I'm doing right now."

"Is it a quilting problem? I can help you with that."

"Not really. I mean it's not quilting—but, let's change the subject to quilting. The other can wait."

"What are you working on? I've got a quilt on my frame a "Robbing Peter to Pay Paul" in blues and greens."

"That's different. If you need some help with

the quilting, though, don't ask me. My stitches are not even and tiny, according to Mother."

"You worry too much what your mother thinks. You have talent in putting pleasing colors together."

"Thanks. I got out the baby quilt I was piecing a while ago."

"Was it for your baby? Oh, Addie, I'm sorry." Mary touched her hand.

"It's all right now. I can look at it without crying. I thought I might as well finish it. One of my friends may need it soon."

"Don't look at me!" Mary Deming blushed. "We can't seem to conceive a baby right now." She looked down at her hands wrapped around the shaking coffee cup.

"I'm sorry, dear Mary. I see it's a sore subject. Do you want another babe?"

"Yes, very much. John, however, seems to be far away in another world. We're not close at the present time."

"Oh, dear." Addie gulped. "I'll pray for you two."

"I'd better go now," said Mary, reverting into pastor's wife mode. "Lots to prepare for Sunday." She bustled out.

Be with my friend in her time of need.

Chapter 24

Mr. Chen's visit came as a surprise. Addie was expecting Liu for another lesson and waited with book, pencil and paper at the back of the bakery. She heard the door swing open.

"It that you, Liu? We have lots to learn today." She looked up and saw a large shape fill the doorway.

"Miss Addie, this is my father, Chen Fu." Addie stood as she noted the lanky frame and single long braid of the man in the doorway. The man held his hands together and bowed low.

"You do me an honor, Miss Addie, to teach my son Liu." He bowed again. Addie noticed his cracked and gnarled hands.

"I am happy to meet you, Mr. Chen. Liu is a fine boy and is getting to be a scholar. His English already has improved. Won't you sit down?" Chen nodded and presented a package.

"This if from Mrs. Chen. Chinese dumplings, her special recipe."

"I'm honored. Thank you." Add stretched out both hands to receive the package and bowed. She set them down on a side table.

"Now, I'll find another chair," Addie found a stool in a corner and brought it out.

"My father come. He tell you something," said Liu.

"First, won't you tell me about yourself and how you decided to come to America. Are you from San Francisco?" She sat down. Chen settled on the stool.

"I am Chen Fu. In my country, China, I was an educated man, a respected scholar. I taught philosophy at the best university in Shanghai. We lived quietly in a small compound with a place for a vegetable garden. We had two children, until one day some soldiers walked by and asked if we wanted to go to America. I said no, but they grabbed our oldest son, Du. He was twelve years old and strong." Mr. Chen looked down at his hands.

"Yes, go on, please," said Addie. "What was Du like?'

"He could play the erhu, a traditional Chinese stringed instrument. He was very smart and also strong from practicing martial arts."

"What happened to Du?"

"The soldiers took our son away and we have never seen him again. I think they put him on a boat to America. The next day they came back and took the rest of us. We three stayed together by locking arms. We were taken to the hold of a big ship heading for San Francisco, we heard. I knew a little English."

"It's very good now," said Addie.

"We crossed the ocean and got sick with the waves and all. In San Francisco, we marched to another ship coming along the coast to Seattle. But, before we got there, Mr. Smith said he needed a new cook and someone to do ironing. He chose my wife and Liu, who was six then. I said I would come with them and do any job Mr. Smith gave me. So, he took me for the lumber mill and here I am."

"I pretend not to know English, so I can listen to what white people say. I learn a lot. They think I'm dumb, but I understand. They say more than they should, because they believe I don't speak the language. It's a good trick." Chen rubbed his rugged hands together.

"Yes, it's a good trick," said Addie. "I wonder if you've heard anyone say bad things and make plans to do something to the workers."

"Why would you like to know?" Chen's dark eyes fixed on Addie's.

"I want to know if anyone is doing something against the law."

"That is a curious question to ask. Are you a policeman?"

"No, and I can't really tell you my purpose. If you decide to help me, you will be on the side of justice." Addie bit her lip.

"Strange." He turned to Liu. "Can I trust her, son?"

"Yes, Father, she is a good person."

"Very well. I do have some information." He turned toward Addie.

"Your husband was murdered."

Addie gasped and covered her eyes. Her hands shook. Just then, Ella Rose ducked in to get a bag of sugar.

"What's this, Addie?" She put one hand on her hip.

"This is Liu's father and he's come to talk about his son's education."

"Well, don't let him stay long. I don't want to have people after me for consorting with foreigners." Ella Rose gave Chen Fu a long glance. "I dare say he's an educated man, though, by the look of his face and his manners." She nodded to him and whirled out of the back room.

Chen stood up. "I will leave now, but I just want to say I heard two men talking in the mill a few days ago. They said Sam Reagan was a person who made much trouble. He had to have an accident. I heard that." Chen bowed and left.

Addie turned to Liu and began the lessons, but a chill invaded her body. She pulled her shawl around her and stifled the shudder that pulsed through her. She dismissed her student early since she couldn't concentrate on the lesson. Before he left, she told Liu:

"Please tell your father to come to me with any information. I need his help."

Addie trudged home in the mist and went straight to her room, deep in thought.

I don't know enough yet. I think I know who is speaking up about mill working conditions. That takes guts in this small town. But reporting them may lead to new crimes, directed by the managers and highest officials of Puget Mill.

Mr. Smith seems to be right in the middle of things. His wife is a social climber, so he may feel driven to bring in more wealth to satisfy her aspirations to move up the ladder of success. Is Martha Smith the spark that's driving this wildfire of crimes?

What about Marcus? He lives in the Smiths' home. Is he involved, either willingly or not? I just don't know. How will I find out more information? My two informants are slow to bring me word of the goings-on in the mill. I can't just walk around in the open. Some people have already started wondering about me. I need to find out and I need to do it quickly.

I know! I can go out at night and observe what's happening at the mill, at least from the outside. If I wear black and stay in the bushes, in the background, I may be able to find out something. Well, that's a real possibility. I think I'll try it tonight. It's not going to rain, either, I think. The clouds are high and thin, for a change. I think there's a half moon tonight, maybe, so I may be able to pick my way around without tripping, like I usually do.

Say, I haven't done anything clumsy for a while.

*What's the difference now? Not so nervous, maybe? No,
I'm definitely worried about this case, about Marcus,
about Hardy and Mr. Smith. I don't think Mr. Ames is
involved. I hope not. I sure hope I don't have to turn in
the top management of Puget Mill Company.*

Addie got up to help Mother with dinner. She
made plans to go after her parents went to bed. On
a dark night, that would be early. If she could avoid
a lecture from her mother tonight, everything
would go smoothly. She'd keep her head down,
do the dishes, her nightly job and excuse herself
to her room. She'd change into her black skirt and
a dark shirtwaist, and then throw the black shawl
over her shoulders.

When the house got quiet, she'd slip out.
I hope this works. I must find out more!

❦

Addie turned the doorknob on the back door.
The hinges creaked.

"Cameron, did you hear that?" Her mother let
out a harsh croak. Addie heard it and froze like an
icicle on the roof.

"Now, Caroline, don't imagine things. You
should be sleeping." The thin walls made it easy
to hear their conversation. Addie sucked in her
breath and waited.

"I thought I heard something."

"Just the normal creaking of a house buffeted by the night wind. Go to sleep."

Addie stood perfectly still, for hours it seemed, until her mother would have certainly gone back to sleep. If only she could stop her constant worrying. Addie tried again and this time the door hinge didn't squeak.

Addie inched around the door and stepped onto the porch. She took each step carefully so she wouldn't trip and fall, or get caught in her long, full skirt. The gabardine rustled, but outside it didn't seem to matter so much. There was nobody nearby to hear it. As she got closer to the mill, the whine of saws muffled any little swish of petticoats.

Addie walked behind a row of waist-high bushes, which lined the path to the mill. As she got closer, she retreated to the shadows. Strong lights lit the mill. The saws' screech sliced the darkness. Men came in and out of the mill pulling log carts. The giant logs were fed into the narrow end of the mill onto a skid and men pushed them along toward the giant teeth of the circular saws.

Sam had told Addie all about the inner workings. Some logs were nine feet in diameter and a hundred feet or more in length. A constant supply was pushed through one end and out came smooth long planks on the other. Several men worked at that end stacking the freshly sawn planks onto palettes.

When the ships came to the dock nearby,

workers used horses to move the palettes toward the open holds. An ingenious block and tackle device hoisted the heavy stacks aboard. Then the ships left for San Francisco, Singapore or Hawaii or some other exotic place. Markets had expanded, but there was a constant supply from the thick forests.

Addie sat on a stump behind a clump of salal grown thick and tall. She waited and watched. The clouds parted in the night sky and the quarter moon emerged like a sleepy night-shift worker from under a warm quilt. Addie yawned. Nothing unusual had happened for the last hour.

Will I have to wait here all night?

Jake Hardy walked out of the side door and looked around. He tapped his foot and folded his arms.

"Hurry up, you two rogues," he yelled toward the bushes. "I haven't got all night."

"Coming, boss." Two men emerged from the forest path maneuvering a log cart. They both wore dark clothing and caps, but when they stopped in front of Hardy, Addie could see one was Tony Esposito. The other man walked with a slight limp. He shoved back his stringy hair with gnarled hands and let out a grunt.

"Hard work, Hardy. But I could use the money. We have ten good logs here."

"I won't ask where you got them," said Hardy. "They're rustled, no doubt. I hope you sawed off the owner's brand from the ends and disposed of them, so there's no evidence."

"Right you are. Me and Tony did it. Right, Tony?" The older man coughed.

"Right, Hall. Pay him what he's due, boss. He works hard for an old man."

Addie bit her lip. She wanted to scream at them all.

Don't you know that's illegal?

"Come to my office after you get those into the mill. Be quick about it. You never know who's watching." Hardy stalked off into the mill. Tony and Mr. Hall shoved the cart and disappeared from view.

You're right, Mr. Hardy. You never know who's looking. It just happens to be a Pinkerton agent. Only I wish I hadn't found out what I just saw. Not the clues I thought I'd find.

What do I do now?

It was getting cold. Addie shivered. Her nose was running. She sneezed. She ducked down into the salal thicket. Heavy footsteps crunched on the path. A hand reached down and pulled her out.

"What are you doing here?" Jake Hardy bellowed at her while holding her collar tight enough to make her cough.

"I can't breathe!"

"Answer the question."

"Just out for a nighttime stroll."

"Like I believe that," said Hardy. "Are you

spying on the doings at the mill? Are you working for someone—you—a scrawny woman?" He grabbed Addie's arm and pulled it tight behind her back.

"Ow! Let go of me. We've done nothing—It's none of your business."

"Oh, so you're meeting a man, maybe? Who?"

"Wouldn't you like to know?" Addie batted her eyelashes and blushed on cue.

"So, you're not going to tell me, is that it?" Hardy released her arm and shoved her away from him.

Addie rubbed her wrist and looked down, shuffling her feet.

"All right, then. Get out of here. Confine your nighttime rendezvous to another part of Port Gamble. Stay away from the mill, do you hear?"

"Yes, sir." Addie acted duly chastised and eased away into the night. A heavy mist settled on her shoulders and head as she trudged back to her parents' house.

Whew. Playing a dumb woman may have its advantages.

Chapter 25

The next day, Hardy stormed into the mill five minutes before starting time. He scribbled names on a stray scrap of wood of workers who came in on time and those who ran in at the starting whistle. Watching each man's motions with an eagle's concentration, he swooped down on his prey.

"Jones, what's the matter? Faster, faster is what I want!" He yelled into the man's ear. The man jerked back as if assaulted.

"Mr. Hardy, I'm not feeling well today. I seem to have a worse than normal cold. I ache all over and my arms are trembling." He held out his hands to demonstrate.

"If you can't work, maybe you need to be dismissed." Hardy placed clenched fists on his hips and planted his feet wide. "What's it going to be?"

"I'll work, sir. Give me a chance. I'll do my share." Jones drew himself up as tall as possible and pushed the log through the whirling saw. He gave a small salute to Hardy.

"That's better, Jones. Don't let me see you

dawdling at your post. Puget Mill pays you good money to do your job."

"I'm grateful for it, too," said Jones, keeping his head down and shoving the boards faster.

Hardy walked down the line. "Who's next? Anybody need a nap or a cup of sassafras tea?" He laughed and curled one lip. All the men kept their eyes down and worked like bees building a hive. The saws hummed, the boards clacked, as the stacks grew higher. Hardy raised his nose up like a lead wolf surveying his territory. Only once did he hear a small cough coming from the crew.

At the final whistle, Jones picked up his feet, like each was a heavy log, and shuffled out the door. He stumbled on his way toward the little hospital. When he knocked on the door, Nurse Lydia Reed let him in.

"How can I help you? You look ill."

"I don't feel well. Thought it was just a cold, but now I feel awful." Jones collapsed. Nurse Reed helped him to an examining table.

"I'll get Doctor Spencer. Just lie here and rest." She disappeared down a short hall and came back with the distinguished red-haired Scotsman following her.

"How ye be, man?" Arthur placed his hand on Jones' neck and felt around. Then he put the back of one hand on the man's forehead. He took a small instrument and looked into the patient's eyes.

"Not good, doctor. I thought I had a cold and

asked to be excused, but the mill foreman kept me working hard all day. Now, I have a hot face, a fierce sore throat and I'm weak as a baby." Mr. Jones coughed after talking so much.

"Let me see your throat." Dr. Spencer took a small flat stick and pushed Jones' tongue down so he could see the back of the throat. "Hmm, red and scratchy, I'd say. Am I r-r-right?" His tongue whirred like a machine.

"Yes, sir. And it's getting hard to swallow. Can you give me something to get me back on my feet? I need to work tomorrow." Jones clutched at his bedclothes.

"I'm afraid, Mr. Jones, you'll need to stay in bed tomorrow. I believe you have contracted diphtheria."

"Oh, no sir, I'll get fired. I need to work." Jones got up on his elbows and eyed the doctor. Dr. Spencer and Nurse Reed put their hands on him and urged him back flat on the bed.

"You can't go anywhere but home. I'll give your wife instructions. Do you have children?"

Jones nodded.

"That changes things. You need to stay here in the hospital. This diphtheria spreads rapidly from person to person. We can't take a chance on your wife or children coming down with it."

"They expect me home tonight. And what can I tell my boss?" Jones' face creased with deep lines. Sweat droplets popped out on his forehead.

"Let me know where you live, man, and I'll send a message to your wife. Also, we'll write your supervisor a note. He won't want you on the line with a contagious disease like this. Now, rest easy and we'll bring you something to help you sleep." Dr. Spencer nodded at Nurse Reed and walked back to his office to write the note. Nurse Reed prepared a tonic of laudanum, and then took down Jones' address before he drifted off to sleep. When Mrs. Jones came tapping on the door, Nurse Reed had instructions for her. Jones would spend two or three days in the hospital sick ward—doctor's orders.

When Hardy received the doctor's note the next day, he wadded it up in his fist and stalked over to the company hospital.

"Let me see Jones," he said. "I don't believe he's as sick as you say." He shoved the crumpled note into Dr. Spencer's face.

Dr. Spencer, a tartan tie around his neck, planted his feet apart and smoothed his wrinkled woolen trousers. "Ya canna see him, Hardy. He's grr-ripped by a fever, and I wil'na have you spreading it throughout the mill."

Hardy threw down the note and raked a gnarled hand through his dark hair. "What am I to do, then? Wait till all the sick ones get nursed back to health? I have a mill to run and a production goal to meet every day."

"You wil'na fire this man." Dr. Spencer

thumped a finger on Hardy's chest. "A disease cannot be helped. It's not his fault."

"Nevertheless, I must keep the saws grinding. I'll have to hire someone else to fill Jones' place until he returns. You'll not chastise me for that!"

"Rrright, man. Do what you must, but I beg you to give this man his job back when he's able to work. Take care ye dinna get it, either."

"We'll see," said Hardy and stomped out. At the end of the day, Stephens and Morgan both reported they felt weak. Hardy sent them to the hospital.

"Come back when you're well, but don't think I'm not checking up on you. I won't tolerate laziness."

Nurse Reed sequestered the three men in the small ward. "Doctor, Mr. Hardy seems to be cooperating with your instructions. Perhaps we can avoid an epidemic."

"Let's hope so," said Dr. Spencer, jamming his hands in his pockets.

The next few days, the patients coughed with wrenching hacks. One of them vomited from the repeated violent contractions of his middle.

All of them burned with fever. It took time to take the temperature of each man multiple times a day. The thermometer had to be cleaned and each measurement took five minutes. Nurse Reed found a woman to nurse the men at night. At the end of the third long day, Nurse Reed walked over to Seaside Place and slumped down on the first chair she saw.

"Can I bring you a cup of coffee, Lydia?" Ella Rose lifted her eyebrows at the sight of the nurse.

Lydia tucked flyaway wisps of hair into her bun. "It's been a busy day, Ella Rose. I'll take that cup of coffee and two molasses cookies, if you have them." She set down her bag and folded her shawl.

"Fred Jones, Luke Stephens and Ira Morgan are all down with diphtheria. We're hoping it hasn't spread and won't spread. It's a serious disease, as you know."

"I do, indeed. It took my little daughter many years ago, and also my wonderful husband." Ella Rose sniffed and let a tear fall. She got two cookies from a clear jar and put them on the saucer with the coffee cup. She set it in front of the tired nurse.

"Did you say diphtheria, Lydia?" Addie slid into the chair next to Lydia.

"That's right. But, let's not start a panic just yet. I think we've contained it by separating out the sick ones."

"You won't get it, I hope." Addie arched her eyebrows, like an awning above her hazel eyes.

"No, I think not." Lydia sipped from her cup and took a bite of cookie. "Mrs. Barber has the night watch tonight, so I can get some rest."

"I've heard people can get heart troubles or even paralyzed limbs." Addie's eyes grew big.

"That's rare, Addie. We're watching the men

and won't allow them to exert themselves for a few more days."

"I imagine the mill foremen and the management must be livid at the slowdown." Addie watched for a reaction from Lydia.

"I don't believe there's a slowdown. I heard Mr. Hardy was hiring replacements."

"That will stir up bad feelings among the workers."

"Oh, he promised to rehire the men, when and if they get well."

"Will he honor that promise?" Lydia shrugged her shoulders.

"Only time will tell. And Hardy didn't want anyone to hear about that promise. I guess it goes against his rock-hard exterior." Lydia chuckled.

"Well, I should go. I'm just so tired." She stood up and dropped a couple of coins on the bakery counter. She threw her heavy woolen shawl around her shoulders and waved as she left.

"The unbending Mr. Hardy seems to have a human streak in his soul, after all." Addie stood up and gulped the rest of her coffee two tables away. "That's a wonder I didn't expect."

Addie dropped her coins on the bakery counter, too, and hurried to get home for dinner.

Mother served up an inquisition along with the fried chicken.

CHAPTER 26

"Addie, I'm appalled you are running around town and not tending to business." Mother passed the plate of fried chicken. Addie took two legs.

"Pass the mashed potatoes, please, Caroline," said Father. Mother flashed a smile at her husband and passed the heaping bowl.

"Here's the gravy, too." She passed the gravy boat that looked like Aladdin's lamp. "As I was saying, you are shirking your duty to your family." She eyed Addie.

"I've washed the dishes and cleaned up after dinner every night, haven't I?" Addie's eyes darted over to her mother's.

"That's not what I mean, young woman. You are required to work in the store with your father. You—"

"I work every morning and sometimes afternoons, too." Addie cut into her Mother's monologue. "You know I'm working on a book, don't you? I have to interview people about that."

"You should work there all day—and not wander around questioning people, especially foreigners." Mother bobbed her head.

"How do you know that? Have you been watching me?" Addie's clenched knuckles turned white.

"Now, Addie, just a minute," said Father.

"I've heard reports. Others have seen you. You are not keeping any secrets from me." Caroline Murray kept on the track.

"Who? Who has seen me? I need to know." Addie leaned forward and reached toward her mother.

"Ella Rose is one. And there are others."

"Caroline! You're spying on Addie. She has a job now. You should know that!" Cameron Murray leveled his gaze at his wife.

"Well, Addie should know that her reputation is suffering. You can't mingle with foreigners too much without becoming tainted." Mother looked down her nose and screwed her mouth into a tiny line.

"Mother, I'm writing a book about the history of this place. I do not carouse with people of low morals. Please don't ever say or imply that again." Addie stood up, knocking her chair backward, and dropped her napkin on the table.

"You've always had such strange and ridiculous ideas. Just imagine wasting time asking people about their recollections about a lumber mill town. Humph!"

"Now, Mother, Addie can handle her job and—"

"Mother, I've lived with your unkind criticism

all my life. I will not tolerate it now, because it's unfounded. I am not a woman of loose morals. I am trying to write a book. And if you persist, I'll move out of your home. I'm an adult now and will find a way to earn a living."

"As you wish, Addie. You are a big disappointment to me. I bore you, but your birth wrecked my insides and my chance to have another child."

"You still hold that against me. Surely you know it was not my fault!" Addie's face turned crimson and her voice trilled louder. "I'll be finding a new place to live as soon as I can arrange it." She looked at her father. "I'm sorry, Father, but I can't live under this criticism another minute." Addie jumped up and ran for the stairs. By the time she reached her room, tears were spilling down her cheeks.

Addie flopped down on her bed and covered her eyes with one arm. When the tears slowed, she fell into a troubled sleep. She heard the echo of her mother's words: "You are a big disappointment to me."

When she awoke, it was dark. She reached out to find the lamp and lit it. Her stomach growled. *No dinner. I'm starving.*

But, more importantly, what will I do?

Ask for wisdom. Believe and not doubt. You have not been given the spirit of fear, but of power, love and a sound mind.

I remember all those words from Pastor Deming's occasional happy sermons. But, how can I act with a sound mind when my own mother berates me? Addie wiped her nose and sat up. She grabbed her journal, which she'd neglected lately. And she grabbed her Bible. *I'll write down my thoughts and make a plan. Then, I need to get some sleep.*

Addie slipped onto her knees on the cold floor. *Lord, I asked for wisdom, but I don't know what to do next. I ask now for courage and clear thinking, to solve the mysteries here in Port Gamble and also to solve the break I've had with my mother. Please mend it, dear Lord. I do love her. It's just all the hurtful words—*

"Addie, how are you and your mother getting along? I know that's always a concern for you." Sarah picked up her cup of coffee and warmed her hands. She and Addie were sitting in Seaside Place drinking coffee and nibbling slices of warm oatmeal bread.

"We had a big disagreement last night. I said I would look for another place to live. Now I regret it."

"Would you like to stay with me a few days?"

"Thanks, Sarah. I knew you'd offer. And I accept. Is it all right with your parents?"

"I already asked them. After a few days, maybe you can patch things up."

"I should go to my mother and apologize for my outburst."

"That takes courage."

"However, I need to make her understand that I have my own life to lead."

"But not for a few days. Let your anger cool. Bring your things over to my place after you're done for the day. You can eat dinner with us."

"Thanks."

"How is the new job going?" Sarah picked at some breadcrumbs on her plate.

"It's puzzling. I'll tell you more in a minute. And some things have distracted me lately. Say, I was just thinking of something." Addie sipped her coffee.

"Sarah, what do you think of Pastor Deming?"

"He scares me every Sunday."

"Yes, those sermons about hell and damnation. He describes the pains of hell so vividly I sometimes got sick to my stomach," said Addie, clutching her middle.

"Yeah, 'the flames of hell are burning, and you are dangling your feet close to the fire if you don't repent. I can smell my feet roasting!" Sarah shivered.

"Sometimes, though, Pastor Deming is so much different. He portrays God as loving and inviting—as wanting the best for us."

"I agree. Maybe he was accused of being soft on sin by some of the older folks."

"Or the deacons," said Addie. "But I hope not," said Addie. "I learn something from him every time he preaches an encouraging sermon. It's a bit of Bible wisdom about how to live life."

"Um, hm." Sarah sipped coffee and popped another piece of bread into her mouth.

"I think he's torn," said Addie, "Torn between what he wants to preach and what he's told to preach. It's so difficult to find the truth, but I will get to it."

"Truth about yourself or truth to report to Pinkerton's and Puget Mill?" Sarah whispered over her cup.

"Both, I guess. I'm learning I can do more with God's help. I'm also seeing that if I report labor agitators, they may get killed in a mill 'accident.' That dilemma is not something I really want to face." Addie spoke just above a whisper to her friend.

"I know you'll make good decisions, Addie."

"Thanks. I know you won't tell anyone, either. Right?" Addie squeezed her friend's arm as Sarah shook her head.

"I'm also learning of other possibly illegal acts going on here at Port Gamble. I can't tell you about those, though."

"The project gets more difficult." Sarah gave Addie a smile. "How many more days to finish the project?"

"Fifty-two." Addie stretched her legs. "I wonder what we'll learn this Sunday?"

"We'll find out tomorrow. I hope it's not about singed toes!" Sarah laughed and reached for her bag. "Time to go. I have errands."

"I'll tell my father I'm staying with you."

Chapter 27

Addie looked up when Chen Fu tapped on the window of the general store. It was almost closing time. She glanced around and saw Father helping Mrs. Murdoch get some provisions. Addie slipped from behind the counter and out the back. Chen met her there.

"I have bad news. First, I think Eddie George is ill. He didn't come to work today. He will lose his job, if he doesn't send the boss a message."

"That's terrible. It seems a lot of natives catch our diseases. And often they don't recover."

"Yes. It's the same with Chinese people. It's a big worry. Can you find out about Eddie, or do you want me to go find him across the bay?" Chen's forehead contracted into grooves and his eyebrows arched like winter-dried leaves clinging to branches.

"I guess it's my responsibility."

"No, it is not a good idea. Everyone will know if you do that."

"Eddie must not lose his job. He has a family, I think. I'll go—and we don't want people to know you understand English." She set a fast pace walking down a small hill nearby and onto the flat peninsula where Eddie kept his boat.

As they rounded a thicket of salal, Chen and Addie saw a canoe pulled up onto the bank. The angular line of the prow jutting up and the distinctive paintings of orcas caught Addie's attention once again. She wanted to know how Eddie made it. She wanted him to keep his job. He was a decent man who caught a deadly white man's disease.

Diphtheria—it was a fearsome opponent. It started as a cold and quickly made the throat so sore a person couldn't swallow. A thick membrane could develop in the back of the throat, too, so it was hard to breathe. And then there was the strength-sapping fever.

He should go to the hospital! I'll see that Eddie gets medical attention.

A woman stepped out of the canoe and made a few tentative steps toward Addie.

"Are you Add-ee?" she said. "I am 'Four Baskets,' Eddie's wife. My English name is Happy." She wore a calico dress, but her hair was braided Indian-style.

"I'm so glad to meet you, Happy. Is Eddie all right? Chen said he didn't come to work today." Chen stood next to her and bowed to Happy.

"He is a good worker. He needs to keep his job."

"Eddie is sick. He has a hot face and he can't eat. His throat—"

"What can we do to help you?" Addie stretched out her hands.

"Please tell the boss, Jake, he will come back when he is well."

"Eddie should come to the hospital here. Others are sick with the same fever and sore throat. He's a worker. He can come." Addie's hand brushed Happy's elbow.

"He is too sick, I think. We will just wait for the sickness to leave. I will take care of him." Happy turned to go.

"He must come to the hospital to get medicine." Chen gestured toward the hospital.

"I must go now. Please tell the boss. Eddie will come back soon." Happy pushed off and tucked her skirts under her bent knees in the canoe. She slipped away through the still water and darkening skies.

"Could you tell Mr. Hardy tomorrow morning?" said Addie, turning toward her companion.

"Have Dr. Spencer send a note," said Chen. "I can't reveal I know English to him."

"Is there another native that comes over to work?" Addie asked.

"I'm sure there's someone on the night shift. Bennie, I think. We could get the medicine now and give it to Bennie. He could get it to Eddie by next morning."

"Let's try." Addie trotted to the hospital, arriving just as Lydia opened the door.

"I'm just getting off duty. What can I do for you?" Lydia, the nurse, drew her wrap around her slumped shoulders. "I'm so weary."

"We have an Indian friend, Eddie George, who is sick, I think, with diphtheria. He's at home across the bay at Point Julia too sick to work at the mill. Could we get him medicine to ease his pain?"

"I could give you a bit of laudanum to help him sleep and something to soothe his throat." Lydia's whole body straightened, filled with energy again. She walked into the little hospital. Addie heard Mrs. Barber ask Lydia why she had returned. Addie stood outside, but heard coughing and gasping going on inside. Lydia returned with two small bottles.

"Can he read English?"

"I think so," said Addie. "I can tell Bennie, his friend, what to do, also."

"Then, just follow the instructions, drink water and rest. He really should come here, although I don't know how the other patients would feel about it." Lydia drew herself up and clasped her hands. "I don't know how I feel about it." She gave the bottle to Addie, who slipped them to Chen.

"Thank you, Lydia. You're a decent person."

"I'm a nurse and don't want anyone to suffer if I can help it. Good night."

"Wait. Could you get Dr. Spencer to tell Jake Hardy that Eddie is sick?"

"The doctor would have to see him—examine him." Lydia turned to go.

"You're right, of course. Thanks." Addie spoke as Lydia walked away home.

I will go to Bennie now," said Chen. "I just need to tell you one more thing. Liu can't come for lessons anymore."

"Why not?" Addie's mouth dropped open.

"Mrs. Smith found out what Liu has been doing in the afternoons. He always came after he got all the laundry done. Everything ironed, too. But she forbids him to take any more lessons." Chen's mouth was a slash of ink.

"Why?" Addie shifted from foot to foot.

"It's not proper for Chinese to learn." He spat the words out, a distasteful mouthful.

"That's the reality, yes."

"Chinese people have an ancient culture. In some ways, we are more advanced than here in America." A muscle twitched in Chen's neck.

"I know you're angry," said Addie. "It is unfair. I will find a way to teach Liu."

Chen bowed low. "You are a kind woman. In China, I met a missionary lady who taught our village about your Jesus. Your holy book, the Bible, says, 'A kind-hearted woman gains respect.' I believe this is a wise saying. You have shown this to my family." He bowed again.

"Now, I must hurry to Bennie, so I won't disturb the next shift and draw attention. But I cannot tell

Mr. Hardy Eddie is sick." Chen walked quickly, one bottle in each fist.

Addie arrived at Sarah's house as dinner was starting. Afterward, she helped Mrs. Larson clean the kitchen and then went to the room the family had provided.

Addie pulled out her journal. It was becoming more than just a place to organize the information she had been gathering. She now included personal thoughts and feelings.

Why must Eddie suffer? He's a good and simple man. He needs this job, too. I know the S'Klallam community across the bay lives off the land. They fish and they use the cedar trees sparingly. They only cut what they need and not to enrich themselves.

Addie looked at what she had just written. It seemed more like one of Job's complaints in the Bible. Or maybe it was a prayer. She closed her eyes and thought about Eddie's situation again. *God, take care of him. And help him not to lose his job.*

The Chens' situation was also on her mind. She scribbled a few words.

The Chens were all abducted from China. Here they are, a respected family in their own country, now feeling the prejudice of Americans who are angry they'll lower the wages of workers. But they only do the most menial jobs. Liu is smart and he wants to learn. I must find a way. Mrs. Chen knows something, I think. She lives in the Smiths' household, and Mr. Smith appears to have shady dealings. I must speak with her.

Another note: I should just stick to my assignment! It's my responsibility to find the mill troublemakers and report them. That means telling Mr. Smith and Mr. Ames. The agitators will lose their job—Or they could have an 'accident.' And I have six weeks.

Addie put down her pencil and rubbed her forehead.

Life is complicated.

CHAPTER 28

The following evening Addie attended the book club social. Drenching rain fell from black skies and a fierce wind pushed her along. Addie drew her heavy coat around her and held on tight to the umbrella.

Inside, the gaslights were turned up bright and the radiators hummed. Addie peeled off her soggy coat and hung it in the cloakroom. She put the dripping umbrella in a metal container.

Several people sat in a circle of chairs. Behind it, another semi-circle echoed its shape. Marcus waved to her. She joined him, bringing her copy of the evening's book discussion.

People blew in, each bringing a gust of wind and raindrops. Laura Benson, the schoolteacher, chose a seat in the inner circle. Ella Rose clomped in leaving wet shoe prints. She sat in the second row, the chair creaking as her frame settled in. Sarah Larson searched like a heron looking for fish and found a second-row seat, brushing damp hair off her forehead. Others came and filled the spaces. Last of all, Tony Esposito made his entrance, scraping a chair across the floor as he pulled it out from the circle and dropped his large frame down. He cracked his knuckles and coughed.

"Let's begin," said Laura Benson. "Tonight, we hope you've all read *A Study in Scarlet* by Arthur Conan Doyle. Mr. Doyle has created a new kind of character that's most interesting. He's a detective. But, more than that, he's a rare kind of detective. He's someone who sees what others don't and solves difficult cases. Our first question of the night is, who is that detective?"

Sarah's hand shot up. "Sherlock Holmes."

"Yes. And every good detective needs a helper. Who's that, Tony?" Laura held out her hand toward him.

"Dr. Watson. Everyone knows that." Tony leaned back until the front feet of the chair lifted off the floor.

"Of course. Now, can someone summarize the crime to be solved?" Laura looked around, smiled and waited.

"There are confusing clues," someone ventured.

"There was a body."

"A mysterious woman," said Tony, raising one eyebrow.

"And police who reach the wrong conclusions," added Marcus.

Comments flowed and everyone contributed bits and pieces. Laura Benson kept asking questions, shaping the discussion and drawing out the right information. At the end, everyone breathed a sigh that sounded like contentment.

Mary Deming entered at that point with a big enameled pot of steaming coffee. Two other ladies cut pies and put pieces out on plates. The discussion circle broke apart and each one moved their chairs into groups of threes or fours. Then they filed along the dessert table and took something from the selection of apple, raisin or blackberry pies. Marcus guided Addie by her elbow through the rush of people. Soon, they each had a piece of pie and a pottery cup of coffee. They chose two seats and immediately Tony dropped down on the third.

"Good discussion, huh?" said Tony.

"I didn't know you enjoyed reading," said Addie.

"There's a lot you don't know about me." He took a big forkful of apple pie.

"Where are you from, Tony?" Marcus asked.

"New York. Went to Public School 10 in Brooklyn borough."

"Really?" Addie looked at him.

"Yeah. Brooklyn is a big place. The Brooklyn Bridge opened six years ago, you know. Lots of people come to New York from Europe, you know. Lots of immigrants--it's a bustling, hustling place." Tony gestured with his forkful of pie.

"My parents came from Maine, like a lot of folks here in Port Gamble." Addie smiled.

"Yeah, well this is about as far as you can get

from New York City or Maine. It's primitive, you know." Tony ran a hand through his pomaded hair.

"Why did you come?" Marcus finished the last of his pie.

"I needed a job, and heard a boat docked in the harbor was bound for the Pacific Coast. I thought that would be a lark, a real, genuine adventure. So, I got on and we traveled a long time. Whew!"

"You went around Cape of Magellan, right, like my parents did?"

"Yeah, I guess. It was so stormy there. I got sick every day. Losing my guts. I just lay on my bed till we passed there. It was tough going all the way up the coast, too. Crazy currents and winds, a sailor said." Tony looked down at his shoes.

"And now, you're here."

"Yeah, I have a good job and I don't want to lose it." Tony raised his chin and his defenses again. "I got the job because I'm a good ball player. Baseball's big in New York City." He got up with a lurch, leaving his plate on the floor. He grabbed his coat from the back of a chair and pushed out the door. A blast of wind and dry leaves blew in.

"I guess it stopped raining," said Addie, kneading her hands together.

"You're upset, aren't you, Addie?" Marcus touched her arm. "Tony can be a bully even when he's trying to be friendly, it seems."

"I think I shared too much about my family. I

feel exposed." She shuddered. "Didn't you feel a menace in the room?"

"He's not tall, but he dominates any place he enters."

Addie clutched her elbows and gave herself a hug.

Marcus got up with a scrape of chairs. "Let me walk you home."

Addie remained seated. "No, I'm all right. I'll just sit here a few more minutes—maybe get another cup of coffee."

"Look, I heard you're not staying at home now. You quarreled with your mother. I will walk you to the Larsons' house. You need to be protected." Marcus took her elbow and nudged her to get up.

Addie nodded and got her damp coat. The two walked outside through a lesser drizzle and finally covered their heads. Marcus reached for Addie's hand and they strolled to the Larsons' house. Addie hesitated and then took his.

"Take care, Addie. Whatever you're involved in, and I think it must be dangerous, be careful!" He squeezed her hand.

Addie smiled at him through wisps of streaming hair. All of a sudden, she leaned on his chest and hugged him. Marcus' arms folded around her slight shoulders. He took a deep breath.

"You're trembling, Addie. Can't you tell me what's bothering you?"

Addie released her grip on him and stepped

back. "I can't. I should not. It's a secret." She clamped a hand over her mouth. "I've said too much. Good night."

Addie turned and ran up the three stairs to the Larsons' back porch. She turned the black metal knob and disappeared inside.

Marcus was left with his mouth open and his brows furrowed. Then, he felt the rain start up again. He shoved his hands into the pockets of his heavy pea jacket and took long strides to reach his room at the Smiths'.

The rain. The rain. Does it always rain here?

CHAPTER 29

Addie woke and rose as soon as dawn unfurled its misty curtain. She unbound her loose nighttime braid and let her caramel hair flow over her shoulders. Taking the horsehair brush, she drew it through her thick hair the recommended one hundred times. Next, she formed a neat braid and coiled it around the back of her head. She secured it with long pins and combed her bangs forward.

Addie splashed some of the cold water in the washbowl on her face. She rubbed her face pink with the rough towel.

I should do something about my appearance. Maybe some lip pomade or rouge for my cheeks. Addie looked at her image in the mirror.

Sam said he liked me just the way I was. That made me feel good, accepted and just right. But, now that I know Marcus, Do I want to be pretty for him?

Addie's eyes opened wide. Her mouth dropped open.

Do I like him that much? I know almost nothing about him. And since he lives at the Smiths, can I even trust him? Is he working for that evil man?

He seems to trust me, even though he knows very

little about me, and my actions lately have been erratic.
She clenched her fist.

No, I'm not ready to love again. It's not possible!
I have nothing to offer. My mother thinks I'll never
amount to anything. Pastor Deming, that Hell and
brimstone preacher, never thinks any of us are worthy,
either. We are all bound for perdition. Deserve it.

Addie went over to her little side table and
wound the alarm clock. It was only six-thirty
and still not fully bright. The dark clouds hung
overhead again. She picked up the Bible and lit the
lamp. Sitting on the bed, she thumbed through the
gold-edged pages.

Do you accept me, God? Am I important in your
eyes? Show me the words.

Addie kept flipping back and forth and reading
a few words here and there.

She looked through the Psalms, a journal of
David and others' hopes and despairs. But nothing
caught her eye. She kept turning toward the end
of the Old Testament and finally let the pages fall
open at Zephaniah. She read the words:

> The LORD thy God in the midst of
> thee *is* mighty; he will save, he will
> rejoice over thee with joy; you will
> rest in his love, he will joy over thee
> with singing.

Tears welled in her eyes. Addie let them roll

down her cheeks. She closed her eyes and pictured God loving her, singing to her that she was beloved. That she was worthy of love and respect. All those things she needed deep inside herself.

Someone rapped on her door.

"Addie, time for breakfast. What's keeping you?" Sarah's voice came through the oak door.

"Sorry, I'm coming." She dabbed at her cheeks with some water and opened the door to the new day. Smells of bacon frying and coffee perking on the stove filled her nostrils. She smiled and ran down the stairs.

"What's your plan for today, Addie?" Sarah passed her a plate of toast. Addie grabbed one and scooped a mound of raspberry jam onto it.

"Mr. Chen said he wouldn't do it, so I feel I have to go to the mill and tell Jake Hardy that Eddie George is sick with diphtheria. And I dread the task. And I don't want Hardy to know Chen understands English." Addie took two over-medium eggs and slid them onto her plate. She sprinkled them with salt. Then she helped herself to some bacon.

"Is that your responsibility? Won't it seem odd to Mr. Hardy?" Mrs. Larson turned around at the stove and looked at her for an answer. Mr. Larson looked up from the paper he was perusing.

"I have to take that chance. I don't want Eddie to lose his job. Keep me in your thoughts this morning." She bit into the toast, then stopped.

"Please don't say anything to anybody, especially my mother."

"We will, dear, whatever you decide," said Mrs. Larson, bringing the speckled enamel coffee pot to the table. "I'm sure all will work out." Mrs. Larson poured the dark liquid into everyone's cup. Mr. Larson rattled the paper into alignment and folded it into his lap.

"Good coffee, honey," he said to his wife. "It really gives me the gumption to face another day." He lifted his cup in salute to her and took a big gulp.

"The mail ship from Seattle is coming in today. So, I'll be busy with that." Sarah dabbed at the golden yolk on her plate with a bit of bread. "Good bread, Mom."

"So many compliments today. I'm honored." She beamed at everyone.

"I love your raspberry jam, Mrs. Larson," said Addie, and took a bit more for a second slice of toast.

"Thank you, Addie. We enjoy your company, but I do hope you can resolve your differences with your mother soon. It's not good to have conflict in the family." Mrs. Larson patted Addie on the shoulder.

Addie nodded and continued eating. "I hope I can," she said.

"I'll be making more bread today," said Mrs. Larson.

"My favorite day of the week," said Mr. Larson, smacking his lips.

"Now get going, everyone. It won't get done with you sitting here." Mrs. Larson gathered the plates from the table. Sarah grabbed her last bit of toast and stuffed it in her mouth. Mr. Larson slurped his coffee.

Everyone pushed away from the table and found their belongings. Soon, hats and coats donned, they ventured out into the day.

Addie looked up to see what the clouds brought today. They had parted and melted away. Addie walked with purpose toward the mill. The work shift had already started. She hurried. Mr. Hardy would be fussing and steaming by now if Eddie wasn't there.

"Wait a moment, young lady." A gruff voice called to Addie and a heavy hand tapped her on the back. She swirled around.

"Mr. Hall. What can I do for you? I'm in a hurry to get to the mill."

"I bet I know the reason. It's to report that Eddie George has diphtheria, right?"

"How did you know?" Addie's eyebrows flew up.

"Two reasons. I heard you talking about it yesterday with that Chinese man."

"You were listening!"

"You're not keeping your secrets very well. Word is spreading that you're up to something."

"W-what?" she sputtered.

"It's true. You sure don't guard your voice in an open area. Anybody could hear you, and some have, including me."

"What's the other reason?" Addie jammed clenched fists on each hip.

"I went to visit him yesterday—Eddie, that is."

"You did? Why would you do that?" Addie's eyes locked onto the old man's face.

"I've no reputation to protect, and, besides, I feel like I owe the Indians some assistance, after all the fighting and killing I've seen in the Army."

"I'm amazed."

"So, I'll go to Jake Hardy. He's a hard man, and it would not be good for you to venture into the mill. Doesn't he have a hair-trigger temper?"

"So I've heard." Addie put her hands back in her pockets. "Why would you do this for me?"

"I know you are working on something important. I want to help. Besides, you remind me of what my daughter might be. The daughter I never knew." Frank Hall looked down at his scuffed boots.

"You're a dear man, Mr. Hall." She kissed him on the cheek. "Why do you steal logs?" Addie looked him straight in the eyes. The old man blushed and drew a gnarled hand over his face.

"How did you find that out?"

"I know how to get information."

"Addie, I'm desperate for money. My Army

pension is meager. I'm a gimpy old man. Wounded in the Indian Wars. I cash my monthly check and buy a few staples to live on. The rest of the month, I have no money. Just wanted to get a little cash."

"What you're doing is against the law. It's stealing."

"Listen, Addie. Arrest me if you want. Right now, I'm going to the mill to help a young woman I admire."

Frank Hall trudged toward the mill, holding one hand on the cheek Addie kissed. He straightened his posture and strode with his best gait, one knee hitching with every stride.

CHAPTER 30

A week later, a familiar voice called to Addie as she entered Seaside Place.

"Addie, come over here a minute." She moved toward the speaker.

"Mr. Hall, hello. Do you have any news for me?" Addie removed her coat and slid into one of the chairs at the table.

"Here, take a cookie first." Frank Hall pushed a plate of sugar cookies toward Addie. She took one and bit into it.

"This the second time I've been here this month, so you know it's something important. I've been skulking around near the mill and pretending to fall asleep on a stump. It's not easy watching people when my eyes are supposed to be closed." Hall chuckled. "Anyway, there's trouble in the air."

"Yes?" Addie leaned forward.

"Oh, first I should tell you what happened when I went to the mill the other day for you. I slowed as I got to the door and poked my nose into the dusty operation. Hardy was indeed making his ire known. His voice bellowed above the buzz of the saws.

"'Where's that no-good Eddie?' he said. 'He's lost his job now! This is the second day he's failed to show up.' Hardy paced along the production line. All the workers kept their heads down, except Chen. He looked about ready to say something, then someone spoke up."

"'Remember, Hardy, I told you he's sick.' It was some guy I didn't know. Hardy raised the back of his hand to slap the man into silence."

"That's when I sauntered in, hands hooked in my belt loops. 'Hardy!' I yelled."

"'Who on earth are you?' said Hardy. He curled his lip and marched up to me like I'd invaded his domain."

"I introduced myself. 'Frank Hall. How do you do?' I held out my hand, but he ignored the gesture."

"He just said, 'What are you doing here?'"

"I explained my reason for coming. 'Got a message for you. From Eddie George. I saw him last night. He's got the fever and aches. Voice scratchy and throat puffed up like a dead fish. He's got diphtheria, no doubt.'"

"Hardy said, 'First, I don't see why I should believe you. And second, I need a certificate from Dr. Spencer. Without that, Eddie loses his job-- tomorrow, without fail. Now, get out of here. You'll hold up our production—already have.' Hardy turned on his heel and plunged into a haze of sawdust. And that was that."

"'Thank you, sir,' I said, and got out of there."

"Thank you for doing that," said Addie. "Do you have anything else to tell me?"

"I heard Dr. Spencer sent a letter soon after I left. Still hadn't examined Eddie but said since so many of the other men had contracted diphtheria, he guessed it was a good bet Eddie had it, too. Another bit of news: a few of the men have been grumbling and talking among themselves at the mill. You know, they were plotting to get even with that mean foreman."

"Hardy?" Addie brushed crumbs off her calico blouse.

"Yeah, I heard that name a lot during the grumbling. Well, it's seems the men decided to strike."

"When?"

"On Thursday, and if necessary, on Friday."

"What do they plan to do—walk off the job—or carry signs?"

"Both, I think. They're tired of the killing pace of the work and the constant danger."

"Who started the idea?"

"Several men—a couple of Irishmen and a Swede—Jensen, I think was his name."

"Does Hardy know about this yet?" Addie rubbed her eyes and then her neck. "There could be a confrontation. In fact, I think it's highly likely."

"Report the men. It's your job, isn't it?"

"How do you know that? I wonder who else knows."

"I heard you talking. You should be more careful." Addie gulped and stared at him.

"You didn't tell me the Irishmen's names."

"Flanagan and O'Malley." Hall gazed at her.

"If I report them, they may end up dead or maimed."

"That's not your concern. Do your job." Mr. Hall leaned back and dunked his cookie into his coffee.

"It's like issuing a death warrant," said Addie. "My conscience hurts." She made two fists in her lap.

"But your job demands it. Quite a dilemma."

"What would you do?" Addie looked into the old soldier's warm brown eyes.

"You have to decide what side you're on, Addie. Either turn them in or quit your job. You can't play on both teams." Frank Hall clunked his coffee cup down and got up.

"Wait. Those are two terrible choices. Isn't there something else I could do?"

"You have the good sense to figure this out, Addie. I'll talk to you in another couple of days." He patted her on the back. "Call on me anytime if you need help. Oh, and some good news—Eddie is back at work."

"Already? I hear the fever leaves you weak as a newborn." Hall shrugged his shoulders.

After Hall left, Addie sat for a long time, supporting her head with elbows on the table. *I'll talk to Mr. Jamison about this. He'll understand.*

With that decision made, Addie tripped out of Seaside Place. She didn't take time to talk to Ella Rose, so she wouldn't have to lie to her. Ella Rose seemed to know a lot, anyway. She bumped hard into a man bundled up in a heavy wool jacket.

"Oh, sorry," she said, and then saw it was Tony Esposito.

"Aren't you the gadfly?" he said. "I see you everywhere." He shoved his hands deeper into bulging pockets.

"I could say the same about you. Sometimes I get the feeling you're following me." Addie's eyes drilled into his. He returned the stare.

"I'm just doing my job." Tony said, holding his hands out to the sides.

"Well, you're not going to scare me. I have things to do, also." Addie set her mouth as firmly as grout between bricks. She took long steps to put some distance between her and Tony. When she didn't hear his heavy steps behind her, she relaxed her pace.

Addie came to a Douglas fir tree, fragrant from the just completed rain. She took a big breath, inhaling as much clean air as she could. The whole world smelled spicy clean, scrubbed by the plump rainclouds. The sun struggled to warm the remains of the day. March was fickle—wind and rain one minute and bright sun the next. She looked out toward the bay. A ray of sun hit a gray cloud and an explosion of color spread out. Well, it was more like a pathway of striped color—a vivid rainbow!

It's a promise. A rainbow always meant something good was coming.

I should go see my mother. Maybe we could talk.

Addie walked to the general store to work the rest of the afternoon. Five customers milled around the counter where her father was standing. He looked up and flashed her a strange look.

Addie grabbed her apron. "Whom may I help next?" she said to the people waiting.

"Well! Finally, Addie is here. I declare I've never been kept waiting this long." Mrs. Sloan puffed her rosy cheeks in and out.

"I'm so sorry. What may I do to help you?" Addie put the prettiest smile on her face she could muster and folded her hands in front of her, waiting.

Mrs. Sloan gave her the list of items she came to purchase, and Addie promptly went for them all. She slid them into Mrs. Sloan canvas bag and tallied the total.

"Here's a peppermint for your trouble. We promise to do our best next time not to inconvenience you." She dropped the candy into Mrs. Sloan's hand and took the coins she offered as payment.

"Don't think I'll be lenient just because I helped

you with your trouble a few months ago, Addie," said Mrs. Sloan.

"No, of course not." Addie dropped another peppermint in the bag.

"I do hope you're better, dear," she said. Addie nodded.

Mrs. Sloan left with the semblance of a happy demeanor as she walked out.

"You're a miracle worker, Addie," said Henrietta Laing, the next person waiting, "I've never seen Mrs. Sloan happy before. Now, here's my list." Addie and her father took turns filling orders for the women needing their last-minute things for dinner. When they were all gone, Father and Addie leaned against the counter and let out big sighs.

"You came at just the right time, daughter. I thought the ladies were going to prod me with their umbrellas." He laughed.

The doorbell jingled.

"Addie. It's you! I haven't seen you for days."

"Mother, how are you?" Addie stiffened her spine.

Caroline Murray swayed into the store, her black gabardine skirt swishing.

"I've certainly missed you, Addie. Nobody to help with the daily chores."

"Is that all I mean to you? A servant to do the menial work?" Addie colored and took a loud breath.

"I didn't mean it to sound that way. But you do have a duty to your parents."

"Mother, I was a married woman with a home of my own until recently."

"So, you don't care to honor your parents?" Mother sniffed and wiped her nose with a handkerchief.

"Now, Caroline—" said Mr. Murray.

"It's all right, Father. Mother and I will never agree on most things. I just hope that she can see I need to find my way in the world." Addie gazed at her mother.

"Humph." Mother turned around and headed to the canned goods display.

"Addie, we both love you and want the best for you. You are always welcome to return home." Father came close to her and whispered. "I just hope that you and Mother can find some common ground. You're always butting heads." He patted her arm.

"I don't know when that day will come," said Addie, going for her coat, "but it's not going to happen yet." She pecked his cheek and hurried out the door.

"Goodbye, Mother. I do love you. When will we be able to get along?" Addie walked out without waiting for an answer. She soon arrived at the Larsons' house.

Well, that rainbow didn't portend what I thought it would. They're just wisps of color that disappear in a blink. And the world remains gray.

Chapter 31

"Caroline, aren't you sorry?" Mr. Murray looked at his wife under a furrowed forehead.

"What do you mean?" Caroline swished around the store and turned to see him.

"Must you always speak harshly to Addie? You'll lose her love if you don't change your ways." His neck muscles tightened.

Caroline stopped her mincing walk in front of the counter. She held out her hand and brushed some dust off a shelf.

"I haven't changed the way I speak to her."

"That's the problem. You just don't realize it. You criticize Addie's every decision and action. Why do you do it?"

"Addie has been a disappointment to me," Mrs. Murray said.

"Why? She's a delightful young woman."

"She married Sam in such a hurry. I wasn't ready for that."

"A little impulsive, but they were well suited to each other."

"I guess so. She seemed happy." Mrs. Murray hesitated.

"It goes back farther than that, doesn't it?" Mr. Murray moved closer to his wife.

"Y-yes. Addie was a big baby. When she was born, she just tore up my insides. I could never have another baby—no boy for you." Caroline Murray wiped her nose.

"My dear, I don't need a boy to be happy. Addie is full of spunk. She's interested in so many things and is always trying to help people. She's a big help to me in the store, also. She has a head for business." He grabbed Caroline's hand.

"Truly? You're satisfied with life?"

"Completely. I have a loving wife and a very likable and responsible daughter."

"Cameron, I feel ashamed. All these years I worried I wasn't a good enough wife for you. I hadn't given you a son. I guess I blamed Addie— made her the reason for my discontent." She leaned against his shoulder.

"Can you two patch up your differences? Talk it out, reach an agreement?"

"I've criticized her all her life. I don't know if I can change." She looked up at her husband. "I did it for her good. Will Addie forgive me?"

"Ask her. Find a way to show her you approve of her."

"But she rankles me. She's so different—not a ladylike young woman. She never was. She's doesn't conform like a proper lady."

"Is that so bad? She's adventurous and loves the outdoors."

"She's more like a boy that way." Mrs. Murray dropped her mouth. "Like a boy—for you. But she's a girl—for me." She clasped her hands together. "I'll find a way to encourage her womanly traits." Mrs. Murray grabbed a piece of paper and wrote a quick note. Then she quickly moved toward the door.

"Now, Caroline. Don't carry this too far. One thing at a time—" But his wife had already gone out the door.

Outside, Caroline Murray was all business. She straightened her clothes, adjusted her hat and draped her shawl around her shoulders in a sweeping gesture. Then, she turned toward the Larsons' house and took a big step.

I don't know if Addie will be there, but I'm sure Anna Larson will be. Why, it's getting time to prepare supper.

❦

Addie burst into Anna Larson's kitchen with such force the woman dropped the spoon she was using to stir the soup.

"Goodness, Addie! What's the matter?" Mrs. Larson wiped the flour off her hands and listened. Wonderful smells filled the warm kitchen. Addie stopped to breathe it in.

"What is that heavenly aroma? It's pungent and peppery, and a little like lavender."

"It's my cardamom bread, dear. You'll have to have a slice when it's done."

"I can hardly wait!" Addie breathed in the spicy aroma again and rolled her eyes.

"Back to the question. What's troubling you, Addie?"

"I just saw my mother in the general store. It was not good. She ridiculed me again. Always! I never want to see her again." Addie slumped down in a chair and covered her face.

"There, there, dear. Let me get you a cup of tea. Maybe you'd like to go to your room and rest." She nudged Addie to move down the hall. "I'll bring your tea in a jiffy."

Anna clucked her tongue and put on the copper teakettle. In a few minutes it whistled it was ready. Anna spooned some tealeaves into a delicate teacup with roses on it.

"Chamomile should help her settle down," murmured Anna Larson, as she placed a cookie on the saucer and then carried the aromatic brew to Addie's room.

"Thank you, Mrs. Larson. Sorry for the outburst. I was just so stunned," said Addie, accepting the warm offering.

"Rest a while and I'll keep everyone away." She waved and closed the door with a quiet click.

Addie sipped the daisy potion and began to

yawn almost at once. She curled up on the bed and drifted into sleep. So, she didn't hear her mother's knock at the door.

"Who could that be at dinnertime?" said Anna Larson.

"I'll get it, Mother," said Sarah. She opened the door to Mrs. Murray.

"Sarah, I understand Addie is staying here. I wonder if I might see her for a few minutes?" She stepped into the covered stoop to get out of the drizzle.

"I'm sorry, Mrs. Murray. She's sleeping now. She came home upset and sick."

"I'd hoped to apologize and make amends. I fear I was the one that upset her."

Mrs. Larson came to the door. "I'm afraid we can't disturb Addie now, but we'll certainly give her your message."

"I was afraid of this, so I wrote out a note. Would you give Addie this?" Caroline Murray extended a small envelope to Mrs. Larson. "I'll leave now. Please tell her I urgently want to speak to her. She is my daughter, after all." Caroline Murray pursed her lips and drew up her shoulders.

"It will probably be tomorrow before she can talk to you. She needs her rest." Mrs. Larson accepted the note and said a polite goodbye to Addie's mother.

Addie heard the conversation and sat up in bed. When she realized it was her mother, she lay back down and threw a shawl over her head. She let the chamomile tea do its work again.

I need to solve this case—and worry about my own problems later.

Addie fell asleep arranging the pieces of the puzzle in her mind.

Is Tony a bully or a killer? Is Hardy a killer? What about Smith and Ames? I just don't know enough yet.

CHAPTER 32

John Deming adjusted his vest, buttoned his suit jacket and grabbed an umbrella from where it was propped near the doorjamb.

"Mary, I believe I'll go out now and visit with some members of the congregation."

"Could you take the children to school first, dear?" His wife came to the doorway of the kitchen and blew a wisp of hair off her face. Her hands dripped with water. "I need to get the dishes done and get to an appointment in ten minutes." She disappeared back into the kitchen, not waiting to hear his answer.

"Certainly." John rocked back and forth on his feet.

"Daddy, daddy," his little daughter ran to him. She grabbed his knee.

"Let's go, children," he said. "Get your coats and lunch pails."

"Daddy, you smell funny." His ten-year-old boy sniffed at his jacket.

"Don't do that, Johnny. It's some medicine I'm taking." He grabbed each by the hand and ushered them out the door.

"Hurry, Daddy. It's cold. I want to get to school fast."

"Slow and steady, Lizzie." Pastor Deming walked with careful steps. Johnny wrenched his hand out of his dad's and took off down the path.

"Race you to school, Liz-bet." Lizzie wriggled her fingers loose from her dad's hand and raced after her brother.

"Whoa, stop, children." John Deming heard his own raspy voice. He tottered ahead trying to catch up, but the children had disappeared around the big bush at the corner. He tried to increase his speed, but his feet wouldn't move. His face felt hot, but his fingers cold and clammy. His arm tingled. He lifted his foot with all his might--and tripped on an exposed tree root. *Why am I dizzy? Am I falling?*

The ground hit him in the face. His nose exploded in pain. Something wet was coming out of it. He felt it with his hand and withdrew blood-drenched fingers.

I'm bleeding! What should I do? His head seemed wooden. Deming rolled onto his side and pushed himself to a sitting position. He scratched the top of his head.

How did I get on the ground? Why am I even here? His head was full of mud—quicksand that sucked all sense out of his brain. *I hear children yelling to each other. Children? Was I supposed to take Lizzie and Johnny to school? I guess they must be there. They're not here with me.*

His body seemed incapable of sensation. He slumped over again.

I'll just lie here a few minutes,

❦

Mary Deming threw a shawl over her shoulders and rubbed her hands together. They resembled lobsters in color and slugs in texture.

Where are my gloves? She made a quick search of the hat rack and found nothing.

Oh, well, Addie will understand. Mary ventured out into the chilly morning. She hid her sore hands under folds of her woolen shawl. She dashed over to Seaside Place, entered and saw Addie was already there.

"Sorry, I'm late. Had to get the dishes done." Mary slipped onto a smooth chair. "What shall we have? I'm starved—didn't eat breakfast."

"Me, either. How about a slice of blueberry coffee cake?" Addie rubbed her hands together and raised her eyebrows.

"Sounds great—and make it a large piece, Ella Rose," she said to the older woman who clumped up to their table.

"Right you are, dears. It's good. I hear there's a great cook here at the bakery." She winked and went back to fill their order.

"What's new?" said Addie to her friend Mary.

"After that episode at church last week, I worry

constantly about John. He's walking a tightrope. He's not steady on his feet and he's not steady in his mind, either."

"What do you mean?" Addie leaned forward.

"Something's wrong. He's distant. His thoughts are far away. Or maybe he's suffering some illness. Dear God, I hope it's not a brain tumor!" Mary covered her face with both hands. Addie reached forwarded and patted Mary's shoulder.

"Don't despair. Let's think of a plan. Is he taking any medicine? Has he been to Dr. Spencer? Has something happened at church to unsettle him?"

Mary dropped her hands into her lap. "I guess I could go talk to Dr. Spencer or Lydia, the nurse."

"Start there, and get some soothing balm for your chapped hands, too. And let me know what you find out, Mary. I—"

"Something's happening outside. Come look," said Ella Rose. She walked over to the front display window and peered out into the mist. "Someone fell down."

"Who is it?" Addie joined Ella Rose to get a look. "Looks like—"

"John!" Mary Deming grabbed her shawl from the chair and dashed out. "I'll pay you later, Addie." Her legs pumped as fast as she could make them go.

"Deming, can you hear me?" The voice came from another world. John moaned and swiped at his nose. Pain hit with full force.

"Deming! Wake up!" Strong hands shook him. His teeth rattled and crashed in his head. John opened one eye.

"Arthur Spencer—Doc! I'm here, as you see." Deming retched. Dr. Spencer turned him on his side. Out came green slime.

"You look awful. What are-ya doing to yourself, John? Are your dear bairns at school?" John opened both eyes and looked around. A group of people circled him.

"Help me load him on a stretcher, Jamie and Rrr-raymond."

"John, John!" Mary Deming arrived in a flurry, her skirts held up so she could run.

"Mairry, we'll take your husband over to the hospital. Check and see if your wee bairns are in school. I think John's been hairre a while. Then meet me at the hospital." Dr. Spencer directed the two burly men to lift the litter Jon Deming sprawled on. He retched again and then moaned.

"Is he going to be all right? How long has he lain on the damp ground?" She wrung her hands and reached for her husband.

"Just got here, Mairr-ry. I was walking to the hospital after breakfast. Can't answer your questions till I examine him." Dr. Spencer touched her arm. "You go and check on your children and meet me at the hospital clinic. Hurry!" He dismissed her with a nudge.

"As for the rest of you, go home or whairr-ever you were headed. I'll deal with Pastor Deming. I'm sure the news will gae oot soon enough." Dr. Spencer's brogue intensified whenever he was agitated.

Dr. Spencer ordered the flannel-clad men to take Pastor Deming to the clinic. Lydia Reed opened the door and bustled around, helping the doctor transfer Deming onto an examining table. She shut the outside door firmly. Spectators trailed away whispering.

CHAPTER 33

Mary Deming raced back from the school and entered the clinic, moving toward the examining room. Nurse Reed held out her hand.

"Just a few minutes, Mary. Doctor needs to take a look, and then you can see your husband. Find a seat in the waiting room." She shut the door.

Mary sniffed and sat down and tried to compose her hands. She stroked one hand and then the other.

She sat there forever. She heard moans and Dr. Spencer giving instructions to Nurse Reed. The giant saws shrieked on in the distance. Mary wanted to add her own shrieks.

What is wrong with John? I must know!

"Mary." Addie slipped in the door and sat next to the pastor's wife. She squeezed her friend's hand.

"What have you found out?"

"Nothing yet. It's been so quiet in there." She pointed to the examining room. Just then, they heard,

"He stole the logs! He stole the logs!" A man's voice bellowed.

"That's John," said Mary. "He must be

conscious." She ran to the door and put her ear to the keyhole.

Dr. Spencer talked in soothing tones.

"Who stole the logs, John?"

"He stole the logs." A pause and retching noises, and then another outburst. "Don't push him!"

"Who, John?"

"Help the cripple. Don't push him!"

Mary opened the door and rushed in.

"John, are you better?" She looked at her husband strapped to the table, and then at Dr. Spencer and Nurse Reed. "What have you done to him?"

"Mary, he nearly fell off the table three times with all his flailing around. We had to strap him here to keep him safe." Lydia led Mary to a seat against the wall.

"He's still not coherent. He been babbling for the last hour and just now yelling."

"What seems to be the problem?"

Dr. Spencer took a small bottle out of his pocket. "Have you seen this before, Mary?"

"No. What is it?"

"Chloroform. Used for an anesthetic while doing surgeries. We found it in one of John's pockets."

"Why on earth would he have that? I mean, I guess he might use it when he stitches up hands and fingers that come too close to the saws."

"That's what we figured," said Dr. Spencer. "But why does he carry it around?"

"I have no idea."

"Has John started acting differently lately?"

"What do you mean?"

"Any strange behavior, unsteadiness on his feet? Does he fall asleep at odd times? Does he say strange things?"

"Yes, all of those." Mary gasped. "Is that because of the chloroform?"

"Has he been under a lot of extra pressure lately?"

"Oh, you mean the deacons pressuring him?"

"To do what?"

"Preach hell and damnation sermons. That just isn't his nature."

"Have you smelled anything on his clothing?"

"A sweet, cloying scent?"

"That's it." Dr. Spencer looked at Nurse Reed. He turned to the pastor's wife.

"Mairr-ry, your husband is verra sick. It was a battle to brring him back to consciousness these past two hours. I believe your husband has been using chloroform to dull all the cares of his pastorate. He most likely is become addicted to the horr-id substance."

"What? That can't be true. He's a good man—upright and moral." She sobbed.

"The habit starts soo innocently and by the

time it takes hold, it's got a grip on a pairson that is fierce. He needs help, Mairry."

"No! I won't believe it." Mary stood up. "I want to take him home. I can nurse him back to health. I can cure him." She lifted her chin and looked at her John.

"That's nae a good idea. He needs treatment. I've haird'o places you can go to cure vicious habits."

"He's a Christian man. He'll overcome it by willpower and prayer."

"It's an evil liquid. Its power is fearsome. There be nae shame in getting treatment."

"It would ruin his pastoral career—his reputation would be destroyed."

"I'll never make it public. Neither will Nurse Reed. Wilya, Lydia?"

"Never."

"No. I want you to release him to me. Now." Mary Deming set her chin and flashed flinty eyes.

"Well, you'll have to wait a bit. I don't think he can walk mare than a couple of steps. And he claims his limbs are numb."

"Of whom are you speaking?" John Deming propped his body up on one elbow, struggling with the straps that held him, and looked at all of them.

"Oh, darling. You're better." Mary moved in close and circled his shoulders with her linked arms. She planted a kiss on his cheek.

"Of course, I'm fine. Just had a long nap--and strange dreams. Such clear and sharp images raced through my brain. Extraordinary."

Lydia Reed released the straps holding him to the table. John sat up and swung his legs over one side. He slid down till his feet touched the floor—and promptly collapsed. Dr. Spencer steadied him just in time.

"Whoa. Guess my legs are a little wobbly. Did I faint? Are the children all right, Mary? Did they get to school? I can't remember if I delivered them."

"Yes, John. They ran all the way to school. They love Miss Benson, their teacher, so much that they always hurry there."

"I'm relieved. I believe I'm ready to go home, Mary. Doctor?"

"John, you hae a prroblem that needs special attention. It's addiction. I strr-rongly advise treatment in a special hospital." Dr. Spencer folded his arms to his chest.

"I'll consider it, Arthur."

"You almost died, John."

"I believe I'll go home and think it over. Thank you. Let me know how much I owe you and I'll come back to pay it." John tested his feet again and they held him.

"At least, come back and let me check yair nose. You'll have a lot of bruising and two black eyes." Dr. Spencer reached for John's shoulder, but Deming turned to his wife.

"Come, Mary. Let's get home before the children are released from school."

"Yes, dear." Mary took his arm. They strolled past Addie on the way out.

CHAPTER 34

In spite of the disturbing event of Pastor Deming's fall, Addie returned to the Larsons, and somehow slept through the night and woke up starving.

I am determined to find out more about Hardy, Smith and Ames.

Addie got up and changed her rumpled blouse and smoothed her skirt, then splashed some water on her face. She unwound her hair and braided it again into a neat crown on her head. Addie thought about Pastor Deming's problem and Mary's denial of it. She had come immediately to comfort Mary, when she first heard of the accident. What Addie had overheard through the open door to the examining room frightened her.

It's obvious that John Deming has an unnatural fondness for an unhealthful substance. I'm sure both Dr. Spencer and Nurse Reed believe it now, too. I've observed the effects, or guessed at them, for a few weeks. I'm sure even Miss Laura Benson, the schoolteacher, wonders why the pastor fainted while walking his children to school. A group of a dozen or so passersby have seen him pass out. Why would Mary choose to deny or even minimize his failing? Does she think she can squash it down and brush it away like a dying fly on the mantel?

Another thing is the random outbursts of Pastor Deming. What did they mean? Anything? Did Pastor Deming hear something? Did one or more of his flock confess something to him? Are his yells just the twisted thinking of his troubled mind?

Someone whose brother is a cripple pushed someone. Where—into the saws? Could that be Marcus? I've never heard he had a brother. I can't believe he would do such a thing. Not him! Can any of Pastor's utterings be trusted? I have so many questions and so few answers.

Addie, intent on her thoughts, braided her hair too loose. It came undone quickly. She sighed and braided it again. By the time she was ready, she could smell breakfast cooking even through the closed door. The aroma of bacon made her stomach lurch and gurgle.

Addie pressed a fist into her middle and chuckled. She opened the door and went up the hall to the kitchen. She heard Mrs. Larson talking and Mr. Larson answering.

"Poor child, she has so much on her mind."

"I don't think I could sleep that long without being ravenous. Make lots of pancakes, Anna." Mr. Larson rattled the newspaper pages and turned to another article.

"You're right, Mr. Larson, I am hungry. The wonderful aromas from the kitchen have gotten me up." Addie greeted the two with a smile and sat down. Sarah dashed in and sat next to her.

"Feeling all right, Addie?" She gave her a light tap on the back.

"I'll be fine. I heard my mother's mother voice yesterday afternoon. What did she want?"

"To talk to you, of course, and, I think, to apologize." Mrs. Larson put down a plate of bacon and a stack of pancakes on the table and pulled a small envelope out of her apron pocket. "Here's a note she left for you, Addie. I told her you were worn out and couldn't see her yesterday. I hope that was all right." Anna Larson looked askance at Addie.

"Thank you for shielding me, Mrs. Larson. I didn't want to talk to her so soon after our spat." Addie curved her mouth in a brief smile. She started to read the note, but Anna continued talking. Addie dropped the note on her lap for later.

"Oh, Arne. Say grace so we can eat." Mr. Larson folded his paper and then his hands as he began a table blessing. They all joined in with their native Norwegian words and at the end Addie said "Amen" with them all. Mr. Larson pushed three pieces of bacon onto his plate with a fork and passed the savory offering. Next, he took two fluffy pancakes and a dab of butter. Lingonberry preserves went on top. He cut a big bite and pushed the sweet concoction into his mouth.

"Mm. Mighty tasty, Anna. This must be a special occasion." He smiled at his wife and then turned to Addie. "Now, young lady, take a big helping. I don't want to see anything left at the end. You need nourishment."

Addie grinned wide and nodded. She already had a mouthful of the warm nuttiness of flapjacks, as her mother called them. "Delicious," she said when she'd finished chewing.

"What are you doing today, Addie?" said Mrs. Larson.

"Finding out more about my project." Addie shut her mouth tight so she wouldn't divulge any more. But her mind planned out a course of action.

They all began chatting and sharing what chores they had to accomplish that day. Mr. Larson didn't work in the mill, so he didn't go quite so early as some. He and Sarah ran the post office and sold stationery supplies in a small shop next to the post office. The little shop was called "Just a Note." Mrs. Larson often contributed some hand-drawn note cards of local scenes.

"Mother, we could use more of the cards that have a picture of the general store. Oh, and some of Seaside Place, too. Those are popular. People like to write to friends and show a bit of what Port Gamble is like."

"How about the scenes of the bay, and the one I drew of that large blue heron?" Mrs. Larson got up and removed the empty plates. Then she poured steaming coffee into all the mugs on the table. "Have to go out today to the store, too."

"Oh, those are nice, too, but we have enough right now," said Sarah. "I think I'd like to make lavender sachets for the shop, too. The ladies would love them. A nice little gift for a friend, maybe." Sarah dabbed at her lips with a napkin.

"Sounds like a fancy city shop, Sissy," said her father, using a pet nickname.

"I'd like to try it. You don't mind, do you, Dad?"

"I don't mind new things. Go ahead. Seems we're all going out today. You know what they say."

"What do they say, Dad?" said Sarah, handing him his cue.

"When the cat's away, the rats dance on the table." He chuckled. "Now, I've got to get to the post office. It's nearly eight o'clock. You coming, Sarah?" The chair creaked as he shifted his weight and stood up. Sarah gulped the last of her coffee and followed after him.

"Bye, Mother. Bye, Addie. I hope you can straighten things out with your mother today. Or at least make a start." Sarah threw a heavy shawl around her shoulders and dashed out the door. Anna Larson busied herself clearing the table. Addie helped by drying the dishes.

The sky outside showed a smear of ashen gray. Addie took the note out of her pocket. She'd had to wait a long time to read it, but now was the time.

Addie sat on a wooden bench in the hall. *What will Mother say to me?*

"What does your mother say, Addie," said Anna, striding into the hall.

"Let me see—" Addie read the message quickly. "Oh, she wants me to attend a quilting bee with her—thinks it will help us if we do a useful activity together."

"She did apologize, right?"

"In her own way," said Addie. "She's not a person who apologizes much." Addie stuffed the note back in her pocket.

"Will you go?"

"Yes. I think I should try to understand my mother better. And she loves quilting. So, I should go with her and try to enjoy it, too."

"So, it's not your favorite occupation?"

"I'm all thumbs when it comes to handwork. Never could make the small even stitches quilters admire so much." Addie shrugged. "Maybe this time I'll be able to."

"Good for you. Go talk to your mother now. It's worth the effort to get along with your parents." Anna patted her shoulder. Addie smiled and went to her room to grab her toothbrush and head to the bathroom. After she was finished, she grabbed a coat and marched to her parents' house, knocking on the back door before entering.

"Mother?" She went to the kitchen. Her mother looked up from the sink, her hands deep in sudsy water. Addie hung up her coat and immediately plucked the dishtowel off its hook. She began wiping the steaming dishes.

"Addie? I didn't expect you. How are you feeling?" Mother stopped and dried her hands on her apron. She made an attempt to embrace her daughter, arms tense and moving mechanically like the hands of a clock.

"I'm fine, Mother. I got your note and would like to go to a quilting bee with you. When will that be held?" Addie let her Mother's arms fall from her shoulders. She hadn't returned the hug, but she did manage a smile.

"It's this afternoon."

Addie grimaced. "I really need to do something first. I hope I can come, but this is vital." Addie darted a glance at her mother's countenance.

"Is it really that important? Can't it wait?" Caroline Murray's lips turned down.

"Yes, it truly is. Something's wrong at the mill, and I need to interview someone." Addie draped her arms one over the other. "Please understand. Tell me where the bee takes place and I'll try to get there."

"One o'clock at the community hall." Caroline Murray finished washing and laying out the dishes and cutlery to finish drying. She drained the sink, wiped her hands and headed for the parlor. "Bring your own needle and thimble."

Addie sighed and put on Sam's old coat.

Before she left, she ventured into her room and pulled the trunk from under the bed. She felt around inside the musty chest and fastened her hands around the cold metal handle. The antique pistol, an 1851 Navy revolver, felt smooth in her hands. She reached for the bullet case, too, and loaded the firearm.

Addie stuffed the pistol in an inner coat pocket and slipped out of her room without a noise. As she closed the back door of the house, she shut away all concerns about the prickly situation with her mother. She strode toward the mill with the beginnings of a plan to enter the mill and look around. The sun shone through patches of clouds and the air wafted a pleasant scent of new growth. As she got near the long, rustic building, Addie heard shouting above the drone of saws. She hurried closer and peeked around a bush. What she saw sent chills through her body.

I can't handle this! Help!

Addie reached in her pocket and cocked her revolver, and then she approached Hardy like a rabbit to a snare.

"Mr. Hardy, I need to see Eddie George."

"Well, he's not here. That other Indian, Bennie, came and told me Eddie's collapsed and is sick as a dog. Not vomiting, but he's stricken." Hardy looked around and paced the sawdust-strewn forest floor next to the mill. "Now, you'd better get out. There's trouble here." As he said that, half a dozen men strode out the door carrying signs:

"Down with danger—up with safety."

"We demand better conditions."

"Less work—More pay."

The men marched around outside the mill, chanting and yelling threats. Hardy strode into his corner office and came back with a big black whip.

"Don't just stand there, Miss Addie, get out of the way. Things are turning ugly." Hardy cracked the whip in the air above the men. Tony Esposito and another Italian—Frankie Russo—came running. Tony plowed into the line, shoving first one then another man. Frankie followed his lead, shouldering the men until one dropped his sign. Tony stomped on it. The man yelled and punched Tony in the face.

I have to do something! I'm responsible to Pinkerton to hand this situation. I have to stop them! This is no time to be afraid.

Addie reached for Sam's revolver, hands shaking. While pulling it out of the inner pocket, it slipped out of her hand and fell. A shot rang out. Tony screamed.

"I've been hit!" He fell and grabbed his ankle.

"Who did that?" yelled Jake Hardy, coiling up his whip. The men scattered and returned to their jobs, leaving their signs on the ground.

Quick as a hair trigger, Addie ducked and snatched her revolver. She stuffed it in the oversize coat. She turned and walked away, red-faced and shaking. She didn't stop until she reached the Larsons' place.

What have I done?

CHAPTER 35

Addie heard the lunch whistle blow as she was walking away from that messy situation. As she suspected, nobody was home at the Larsons' this time of day. She crept into the house and stashed her revolver in the depths of her tapestry case with all her other things. Then she sat on the bed and considered her options. Her mind went over again all the events at the mill.

I'll need to make a report to Agent Jamison. It is time for my second summary of the case. And I'll have to tell him I accidentally shot Tony. I shouldn't have just walked away, I guess. But I'd rather have Jamison examine the case than anyone here. The situation is tense and deteriorating.

Addie took out her journal. She'd brought it with her for this time away from home. She had a section in it for her feelings about her mother and herself, but now she turned to the part marked "Mill Investigation." She scanned it, and then took a fresh sheet of paper.

First, I'll write a report to Agent Jamison. She set forth as clearly as possible the chronology of events. Then she discussed the suspects. This is what Mr. Smith and Mr. Ames had asked for. She warned Jamison that she'd stopped a near-riot but had shot Tony Esposito accidentally. Addie said a bigger riot might erupt soon—within days. She'd have to send the report right away, with the essentials, to convey the urgency of the situation. She sighed and walked over to the post office.

She bought an envelope, sealed the report inside and bought a stamp. Addie took the letter to the *Western Star*, the steam ship waiting in the harbor. She knew the purser and soon found him.

"Milt, are you making for Seattle today?"

"Right you are, Addie. We're just finishing unloading our cargo from San Francisco. We'll be sailing to Seattle this evening. Why?" His Adam's apple bobbed.

"I have a very important letter for you to deliver. Could you do me a big favor and get it to Simon Jamison tonight?" Addie handed him the fat letter.

Milt looked at the letter in his hand. "Pinkerton Agency? This must be something important." He looked into her eyes. "You're not in trouble are you, Addie?"

"No, Milt, but thanks for asking." She patted his ink-smudged hand. "But, if you get that to Mr. Jamison by tonight, I'll treat you to a big piece of pie with whipped cream next time you come through."

"Whew, that's a great offer. I accept. You can count on me, Addie." She gave him a smile and quick hug, and left the lanky youth rocking back on his heels.

Addie walked back toward town.

Have I helped or made the situation worse? I'll need to surrender myself to Mr. Jamison, so I'm probably off the case and out of a job. I mustn't delay.

After she finished with that unhappy chore, Addie realized she just had time to get to the quilting bee. She stopped by the general store and borrowed a needle and thimble from the sewing display. Father was busy with a customer and just waved.

Addie reached the community hall steps just as her mother did.

"Addie, I'm so glad you came. Help me with this big basket of scraps. We're having an exchange—increases the variety in all our quilts and nothing is wasted."

"All right, Mother." Addie grabbed the basket and followed up the stairs. They shrugged off their coats and hung them in the coat closet. Out in the middle of the big hall, the rows of chairs had been pushed to the edges. A huge rectangular frame about eight feet long by four feet wide stood in the center. It held a colorful quilt rolled and stretched between two bars. As the quilting was finished in one long swath, the bar was turned to expose an un-quilted expanse.

"Do you remember that pattern, Addie?"

"Crosses and Losses, isn't it?"

"Very good," said Mother. "I love how all the triangles make star patterns when they're all sewn together. And you can piece them from the smallest remnants."

"I heard it was popular during the Civil War." Addie smiled and sat down next to her mother. She got out her borrowed thimble and needle. She flexed her fingers to loosen them for the task. The chatter of women's voices wove through the air, creating layers of discussion from bits and snippets of talk.

"Did you hear the news?"

"No, what?"

"There was a disturbance at the mill."

"Really, how exciting."

"Someone fired a shot."

"They shot Tony Esposito."

"Who?"

"Tony Esposito is a low-down trickster, my husband says."

"I mean who shot him?"

"Nobody seems to know."

"But they'll soon find the culprit, you can count on that."

"You're right, Ethel, of course."

"There's nothing to worry about."

"But the killer is still on the loose."

"But nobody died, Ethel."

"Oh, that's right. But I'll feel better when that man is safely in jail. This is a peaceful community."

Addie listened with one ear while leaning over the quilt. Her fingers tensed as she followed the chatter. Addie poked her needle through the layers of cloth and batting. With one hand underneath the quilt, she felt the sharp point and guided it into position a tiny fraction of an inch from the first and pushed it upward. She nicked her finger and brought it quickly to her mouth to keep the blood from landing on the quilt. She wrapped her finger with a scrap of cloth until the bleeding stopped. Then she resumed her slow work.

Addie stopped to watch her mother. Her slender fingers worked the needle, pushing the thimble here and there to accomplish it all. Her stitches lined up evenly with spaces between them equal to the actual stitches. She hummed as she worked with quick motions.

"Mother, your work is beautiful," said Addie. "You're an excellent quilter."

"Thank you, dear. I love fine handwork like this." Caroline Murray beamed at her daughter. She looked at Addie's contribution to the quilt. "Just a little more practice would—"

"I know my work's not perfect. It never will be. I just don't have the patience."

"Nonsense, Addie. You're doing—"

"Never mind, Mother. We both know it's not what it should be. I think I'll just watch for the rest of the time." Addie removed the thimble from her middle finger and put the needle through the paper holder she'd brought it in.

Caroline Murray sighed and went back to her work. Addie strolled around the frame, watching over each quilter's shoulder a while, then moving on. After a while, she ventured over to the window and looked out.

The clouds parted and sunrays fell onto a portion of the beach down below the town. Addie remembered then the Indians originally named the place Teekalet, meaning "brightness of the noon day sun." Sun streamed into the community hall windows. Shadows danced across the quilt and the ladies hovering over it. Addie watched a steam ship take on its load of split lumber. Once a log was cut into boards, the workers piled them onto palettes. The stacks of lumber sat in the lumberyard under a roofed but open-sided shed to dry.

Addie noticed several men operating a block and tackle and guiding a stack of lumber into the hold of the ship. Men inside the vessel received the palette and put it in its assigned space. Always the drone and scream of saws and machinery filled the air. Addie turned back toward the ladies as Mrs. Monroe said,

"Ladies, thank you for your help. It's time we stopped for some refreshment."

The ladies sighed all at once and looked up, rubbing their hands and shoulders. Two ladies brought out trays of apple pan dowdy, heaped with whipped cream. The younger ladies leaped up and scurried over to the tables and chairs. Those that remembered their manners helped the older women who stood up and straightened out their backs with care. More than one rubbed and flexed their cramped hands. The tall enamel coffee pot announced by its aroma that coffee was ready. Addie joined them and took a few bites. She listened to the easy talk of the women and relaxed in their presence.

Soon, her mother nodded it was time to go. They gathered their wraps and stepped out the door. The sun now hid behind gray clouds and winds whipped at their skirts.

"A storm is coming. Let's hurry home, Addie." Caroline Murray drew her coat up over her neck and stepped faster.

"Mother, I'm going back to the Larsons'. I'll see you tomorrow."

Mother stopped and jerked her head toward Addie. "You're not coming home?"

"No, Mother, Not yet."

"Is it something I said? I criticized you again, didn't I?"

"It's not that so much. I wish you'd accept me the way I am. I'm not a fine lady and never will be. I'm an outdoor person. I love the woods, the plants and the mountains. I still think I'm able to amount to something, to make a difference in life."

"Doing a man's job? I don't know, Addie. I

worry so about you." She turned. "I do love you, Addie. Please know that. It's just hard for me to accept your current situation. Be careful." She touched Addie's arm and was gone.

Addie trudged toward the Larsons' home, head down, kicking small stones aside. *Mother won't have to worry about my roaming around anymore. I'm sure to get fired.*

CHAPTER 36

Jamison stepped off the boat at Port Gamble and strode up the walkway. It was snowing lightly, unusual for March. Wet flakes stuck to his hat and settled on his shoulders. He frowned and looked around for her.

Addie Reagan had sent a letter yesterday that got his attention.

The situation at Port Gamble had reached a crisis point and Mrs. Reagan feared there would be fatalities if something weren't done soon. A near-riot broke out yesterday. She just happened to be there at the time and tried to intervene, but she dropped her revolver. Dropped it! And shot someone in the foot. She destroyed her undercover profile, too. That was sure!

Jamison shook his head as he replayed the report in his mind. *Who have I put on this case? An amateur? I need to see for myself, and I'll just fire her now. She's compromised the case. She did, however, give me some names I could report to Ames. That will be an unpleasant but necessary duty today. This investigation is a disaster.*

Jamison brushed the snow off his hat and his shoulders. He made for the hotel.

I need some lunch and then I'll look for Mrs. Reagan. I may have to wrap up the investigation myself. How can I explain the events of yesterday to demanding Mr. Ames?

As Jamison strode to the little hotel, he saw someone out of the corner of his eye.

"Mrs. Reagan." He waved to her and trotted over.

"Mr. Jamison. I didn't expect to see you—so soon."

"I hired a boat to bring me here. Is there some place private we can go to talk?"

"I know a quiet place. There aren't too many around here." She led him to a covered gazebo on the hotel grounds. They sat down. He brushed the soggy snow off his boots, shoulders and shook it from his hat.

"Now, tell me everything," he said. "And, by the way, you're fired."

Addie's eyes got big. She raised her eyebrows and gasped. Then, she took a big breath and placed her fists in her lap. The knuckles were white.

"Mr. Jamison, I defy you to describe a better way to pursue the investigation. I have done my best. If you don't employ me at Pinkerton, I'll—open my own investigation agency. Reagan Investigations, that sounds good." She smiled at him.

"Now, don't get agitated," said Mr. Jamison, pacing the floor. "Tell me, why were you at the mill when the disturbance broke out? Why were you armed? Who in damnation did you think you were going to shoot? And why didn't you keep a low profile, like I told you?" Addie took a breath before speaking.

"I just happened to be there at the right—or wrong—time. I was trying to think of a legitimate reason to go there, so I thought I could say I had a message to deliver. However, when I arrived, the strike broke out before I said a thing. And I had to get involved. I didn't want anyone to get injured."

"Then, why did you shoot someone?"

Addie's cheeks turned pink. "Did I tell you I sometimes get clumsy when I'm nervous?"

Jamison threw up his hands and shook his head.

"Well, it's true. I stumble or I drop something." I'm ashamed that I can't always control that. I'm working on it—to remain calm under trying circumstances."

"Well, what happened?"

"I took my revolver out of my pocket and cocked it. I was so nervous, the gun must have slipped out of my hand and discharged when it hit the ground. Unfortunately, the bullet hit a man in the ankle." Addie pursed her lips. "At least, it did stop the disturbance."

"What have you accomplished? You caused injury and revealed your allegiances."

"People don't know I'm working for Pinkerton."

"They know you're snooping around. That's

enough. You've destroyed your effectiveness. Tell me you've solved the case."

"Well, I'm pretty sure Jake Hardy and Elliot Smith are guilty of causing a number of mill accidents. People have been shoved into the saws, causing lots of cuts, lost fingers and several probable murders."

"Your job is to find out the labor agitators and report them to Ames and Smith. What have you done on that front?" Jamison stamped his feet and rubbed his hands together. His breath came out in a cloud of vapor.

"That's easy. I already told you: Jensen, Flanagan and O'Malley. They were leading the strike yesterday. It was Tony Esposito and his friend, Frankie Russo, who opposed them. Hardy, the foreman, of course, was in there trying to break it up."

"So, have you reported this to Smith and Ames?"

"No, that's your job. I want to stay incognito."

"Oh, a fancy word. You're learning the trade slang."

"Okay, undercover." Addie colored and clenched her fists again.

I'd like to smack him.

"I did come to give a report to Smith and Ames, as it happens. I also came to check out the mill situation. You said it's reached a crisis point."

"Yes, it has. I think anytime there will be a

full-blown riot that will be impossible to stop. I could use your help."

"First of all, I'm taking over."

"So, I'm not fired now?"

"You're helping me till this is over."

"It's my case. I know all the details."

"All we have to do to satisfy the big wigs is to break up the labor agitators, arrest a couple of them and everything will fall back into place. The rest of the men will be afraid to protest."

"But, don't you see, Smith and Ames will see that these men—the agitators—suffer a mysterious accident or worse. I can't let that happen."

"You can't stop it. You'd have to patrol the mill twenty-four hours a day."

"We've got to try!" Addie jumped up and paced in front of Jamison. The lunch whistle blew. "Come with me. I want you to meet someone," said Addie.

Jamison followed Addie, his wind-chapped hands shoved into his coat pockets. The wet snow kept falling, creating a soggy blanket of white throughout the settlement. They stood under a tree along the path leading to the dining hall.

The mill disgorged its workers. They sprinted toward the smell of food.

"They haven't eaten since five-thirty this morning. I'll try to get one person to stop for a minute." She scanned the mass of hurtling bodies.

"Chen," she yelled. A thin, muscular man with

skin the color of faded parchment stepped out of the racing men and sauntered over to Addie.

"Mrs. Reagan. You need help?" Chen Fu bowed slightly.

"Chen, this is Agent Jamison, an agent for Pinkerton's Agency." She gestured toward the shivering figure next to her. Chen bowed.

"Who is this Jamison?" Chen spoke quietly.

"My boss."

"Who is this—man?" said Jamison.

"He's my informant?" Addie replied.

"Do you have any information about what goes on in the mill?" He eyed Chen from under his now dripping hat.

"No time to talk now. I must eat. Only have twenty minutes."

"I understand," said Jamison. "But, could you, at a better time, give a statement regarding any illegal activities occurring in the mill?"

Chen hesitated. "I know some things."

"Would you help us by identifying people who are agitating for unions?"

"No, not that, but I would tell about how people are being pushed into the spinning saws." Chen set his mouth in a straight line, his lips blue. He shivered.

"You're cold and so am I. Could you meet me after your shift is over?"

"Yes. I will meet you here at five-thirty. But

hide yourself in the bushes." Chen sprinted off to catch the retreating line of hungry men.

"Let's get out of here. I'm freezing," said Jamison. Addie nodded and matched her steps to his hurried ones. They reached the small hotel in no time. Jamison shook himself all over, a dog coming out of the water.

Addie snickered and backed away from the spray until she could make a straight line to the door.

"I'll order some good hot coffee." She disappeared inside, while Jamison brushed more snow off his clothes and wiped his face with a handkerchief. He parked himself on a chair at the table where Addie sat.

"I need to order lunch, too," said Jamison. "Are you hungry?"

"I could use a bowl of chicken soup."

"That sounds comforting. I'll have that, too, and some bread."

The waitress brought coffee and two cups and then took their orders. Addie smoothed her skirts and arranged her damp coat over the back of a third chair. Jamison stretched his legs out under the table. The warmth of the dining room and its pleasing aromas brought him up short. The anger and frustration he felt over this whole fiasco lost some of its force.

What do I make of this infuriating woman?
"Mr. Jamison—"

"Mrs. Reagan?"

"Just give me the rest of the ninety days to prove myself. I can make good." She leaned forward. "How many days do I have left?"

"About two weeks, I think. I'll have to check when I get back to Seattle."

"I'm so close to solving this thing."

"Well, you've discovered the labor agitators. That's all we were hired to do, remember?"

"You know there's more than that going on. There's a murderer to find."

"Keep your voice down," said Jamison, as the waitress returned with two bowls brimming with noodles and chunks of chicken. The aromas made Addie nearly faint with longing. It took her back to her grandmother's kitchen and the pleasure she had as a girl of dropping chopped carrots into the soup pot. Her stomach gurgled loudly. She punched a fist into her middle.

"Hungry?" said Jamison, buttering a slice of fine white bread.

"Apparently so." Addie took a big spoonful of soup into her mouth. It burned, but she swallowed it anyway with a sputter. She grabbed the bread and took a bite to cool off her mouth.

Jamison laughed and stirred his soup.

"Nervous about something?"

"I don't know where I stand with you," said Addie. "But I'm asking you to come with me to the mill this afternoon. I think there will be trouble. I'll need your help."

"All right, I'll go, but I don't officially approve."

"As long as you go," said Addie.

"I wouldn't want you to drop your revolver again, Mrs. Reagan, so I guess I have no choice." He flashed a crooked grin and then made himself busy finishing the soup.

Chapter 37

Addie's pulse raced as she strode toward the mill. The revolver in her pocket slapped her thigh with every step. She'd retrieved it from Sarah's house while Jamison loaded his Remington revolver. He had a ring lanyard attached to its grip and secured it inside his suit jacket on a button. Addie had to conceal hers inside Sam's oversize coat. It bulged anywhere she put it. At least the slushy rain had stopped.

Jamison followed behind her, but behind bushes on one side of the path. Addie heard his gun click as he cocked it.

Men shouted and jostled one another in the mill yard. The giant saws buzzed. Sawdust floated in a cloud around them. Addie and Jamison looked at each other. He motioned for them to bend down and listen.

"Clear out, you lazy bums. Get back to work," Hardy yelled at the strikers.

"Unsafe, unsafe," they chanted and circled around the entry.

"I'm warning you," yelled Hardy. "Stop or you'll be sorry."

They kept marching. Addie stepped out of the bushes.

"What are you doing here?" Hardy came barreling out of the mill, more concerned now about her than the striking workers. He carried a big whip and let it uncoil at his feet. She flinched.

"I have a message for Eddie."

"Eddie's not here, I told you. He's sicker than before. Maybe dying. Go!"

Hardy raised the whip and let it snap right next to her ear. Addie felt a sting on her cheek as the air parted. She smelled wet leather as it passed by. Hardy rewound it and pushed into the rowdy group. He grabbed at their handmade signs. They pulled back. Snap! The whip sought another victim.

Addie brought a hand up to her cheek and felt a drop of blood. She brushed it aside. She surveyed the scene and noticed where Jamison had set up a position. Addie retreated to the other side of the path and found a large stump to hide behind.

Where was Chen Fu? Was Eddie really at home on his sick bed?

Addie watched the progression of the commotion. Without Tony there, Frankie turned from shoving men and grabbing signs to outright violence. He punched Jensen, the clear leader of the group. Jensen staggered and grabbed his jaw. Blood oozed from his mouth. He folded a dirty bandana from his pocket into one side of his mouth and kept up the heckling.

"Safety first builds trust!"

"More pay, shorter days!"

"Saws kill, fix the mill!"

The workers raised their voices to a roar. Someone stopped the saws just then, so the noise of the yelling spread and echoed through the trees. Addie covered her ears.

Jake Hardy joined in the fracas snapping his whip overhead and when they didn't stop, he snapped it around the legs of a man in the front line. The man shrieked and dropped his sign. Falling to the ground, he knocked over another man. Hardy unleashed his whip through the crowd again. Another scream of pain. The group slowed their marching and muttered to each other.

"Good work, Hardy." Someone clapped him on the shoulder. He recoiled his whip for another strike.

"Mr. Smith, you shouldn't be here." He shot a look at the imposing man in the tailored suit.

"I heard the noise from my house. You'll soon attract a crowd here. Deal with this quickly, Hardy—any way you can."

"Yes, sir, Mr. Smith. I'm using my whip to break it up."

"Can't you do more?"

Addie leaned forward to hear the next words.

"What more can I do?" He looked Smith in the eye.

"Maybe I can help, Mr. Smith." A young man strode up to him. "If Hardy here rounds up the troublemakers, I'll deal with them. You know I will."

Addie's mouth dropped open. She peeked from her hidden position toward the spot she knew Jamison occupied. Jamison was looking, too. He shot Addie a look and gestured with a nod of the head toward the clot of men discussing the situation. Addie cupped her ear to hear the next words, and then motioned she would move in closer.

"Do it quickly," said Smith, "But after I'm gone.

"I'm not going to involve myself in that. That's murder." Hardy stepped away.

"It's not murder. It's just an accident." Marcus Williams whispered to Hardy. "The saws are nice and sharp. I just made sure of that." Marcus turned just enough so that Addie could see his face.

He's gleeful. He actually looks like he'll enjoy pushing people to their death.

Smith lifted his chin in affirmation.

Addie stood up and started walking toward the group.

"How could I have been so wrong about you, Marcus?" she said in a loud voice. Jamison saw and scrambled out of hiding to join her. He held his Remington with both hands. The strikers dropped their signs and ran for cover. They helped the two whipped men limp to safety.

"I arrest you with the authority of the U.S. Government." Jamison took a stance in front of them.

"And who are you?" Mr. Smith spat the words out of a curled lip.

"Remember me? I'm Simon Jamison, Pinkerton agent. And this is Agent Reagan." He motioned toward Addie. She nearly dropped her revolver again. Instead, she made a great effort to grip it tighter and fixed her face into a passive stare.

"You have nothing on me," said Marcus, looking towards Addie. "I knew you were hiding something."

"I've heard enough. You said an accident isn't murder," said Addie, "I say murder isn't an accident."

"No one will take your word," said Marcus. "You're hysterical." He curled his lips into a sneer.

Addie gasped and turned away.

"Shut up," said Jamison.

"Where's Hardy?" said Addie, holding back tears that threatened to undo her. She looked around the scene.

"Here, Mrs. Reagan. I'm not going anywhere." Hardy waved his hand at her.

"I thought you were arranging the 'accidents.' What role have you taken?"

"I needed this job so bad. I had to obey Smith's orders or lose my livelihood."

"Keep your mouth shut, Hardy." Mr. Smith's roaring voice cracked.

"No, Mr. Smith. I'll back up Mrs. Reagan That's what Marcus said. I've roughed up a lot of workers in the mill and looked the other way when some were bumped into the saws. I'm ashamed. I'm ready to surrender myself." He stepped forward and held his wrists together.

Jamison threw a pair of handcuffs to Addie. She snapped them on Hardy and nudged him to the side. Jamison produced another two sets and Addie helped cuff Smith. Marcus tried to run. Jamison sprinted after him and knocked him down.

"You'll ruin my new wool shirt." Marcus thrashed around till Jamison sat on him and clamped the heavy rings and latches together.

"You'll hear from Mr. Ames soon enough. He'll get me out." Smith sputtered and turned purple.

"You're going to the jailhouse here, and I'm calling for extra escorts. You'll be tucked up snug into the lockup in Seattle by nightfall." Jamison spoke to him nose to nose.

"Now, Addie—"

"Call me Adaira. I'm Adaira Reagan, and I assume I've passed my ninety-day probation period, right?"

"Yes. I'm proud to say you are now an agent

in good standing. Good work, Agent Reagan." He flashed his straight white teeth at her.

"At last. Agent Adaira Reagan, my dream job. And I haven't tripped or dropped anything for weeks. Well, a few days, anyway." She lowered her voice so the others wouldn't hear. Jamison grinned.

"Well, escort these criminals to the jail, Agent Reagan."

"Yes, sir. Say, what is your first name, anyway?"

"It's Simon." His ears turned crimson. "Now, go!"

Addie followed orders and pushed the cuffed men forward. Jamison followed along as backup.

The sun broke through the sodden clouds, and the mill workers cheered. Hardy yelled, "Take the rest of the day off and wait for further orders from the management."

The workers cheered again and dispersed in all directions.

"Agent Adaira Reagan, I'll meet you at Seaside Place in ten minutes."

"Yes, sir, Agent Simon Jamison." Addie brushed her long mane back on her shoulders and smiled. *That good day is here at last.*

Chapter 38

Sunday arrived and with it another punishing sermon.

"Do you know where you'll spend eternity? Your sins are many. They are weighing you down. Repent. Confess. Perhaps God will have mercy on you." Pastor Deming took a deep breath and mopped his forehead with a handkerchief. He looked at various faces in the congregation. Mrs. Sloan pursed her lips. Laura Benson's eyes opened wide. Deacon Flynn nodded and his mouth curved up. Many hung their heads. Shoulders slumped to receive the load of verbal abuse he'd delivered already. Addie Reagan narrowed her eyes and gave him an icy stare. Pastor Deming plunged into the battle again.

"The Devil prowls like a roaring lion, seeking whom he may devour." Addie recognized the verses from the New Testament.

"Resist him, standing strong in faith. Turn to God!"

Pews creaked as people shifted in their pews. Deming continued for another twenty minutes, and then closed his Bible. The parson raised his hand high.

"Behold, now is the time!" He slammed it down on the podium. A number of people flinched. Widow Jackson in the back row fainted and was helped out. He looked to his wife, Mary, and nodded. She began the first bars of a hymn, as Pastor Deming signaled for all to stand. It was "Love Divine," not the somber one he had chosen.

He shot Mary a look—furrowed eyebrows and stern face. She kept playing.

The pastor released everyone with a benediction. Pews emptied and the flock scattered before their shepherd could get to the door. Deming said a few words to Widow Jackson. He prayed for her soul, though she didn't request it. Mary Deming collected her things and followed him out, holding Lizzie and Johnny's hands.

"Good sermon, pastor." Deacon Flynn shook his hand. "Keep it up."

"Interesting hymn you chose." Deacon Erickson rocked back and forth on the balls of his feet and walked out the church door.

Mary served a dinner of chicken and dumplings, with a slice of apple pie made from dried apples plumped up in water. The children ate quickly and excused themselves. Mary cleared the dishes and disappeared to the kitchen. Since Pastor Deming did not insist on a stringent keeping of the Sabbath, Johnny found a book to read and Lizzie played with her dolly. Mary went up to their room to lie down and rest.

I believe I'll go to my study and read the commentaries again. He chuckled at the euphemism. To him, this phrase had gradually come to mean indulging in a sniff of chloroform, to his mind a just rationalization. He was doing research—studying. Safe in his study, he opened a new bottle of chloroform and held it under his nose. He laid his head down on the open book.

Sweet relief and vivid images! Paradise found.

After what seemed a short time, he became aware someone opened the door. It squeaked at the end of a long tunnel—nothing to worry about. John Deming slept on.

The next day, Mary Deming decided to keep an eye on John's daily habits. What she saw yesterday had disturbed her. She peeked into the study and saw John sprawled over several large reference books on the top of his desk. He had a silly look on his face, as though retreating into a far corner of his mind. And his mouth hung open. Drool oozed from his mouth and had pooled in the crack of a book's spine. Mary dabbed at it with her handkerchief and pushed John's mouth closed.

This is not the John Deming I married. I must do something.

CHAPTER 39

Addie entered Seaside Place and greeted Ella Rose.

"Sorry I haven't been here for a while."

"Addie, I do apologize. I should be hanged for kicking you out of the backroom. I'm ashamed I didn't want you to teach your student there." She looked down at her flour- sprinkled shoes.

"I don't know why I'm always such a crusader. And I laid that burden on you."

"I know why. You champion the underdog because you've been one." She leaned over to hug her friend.

"Say, did you hear? Eddie George died."

"What—oh, no!" Addie covered her mouth. "How?"

"Had a relapse after his bout of diphtheria."

"He went back to work before his was totally well, I think. What will his wife do?"

"Don't know. I guess their people will take care of her and the baby." Ella Rose shifted her sturdy shoes. "Anyway, go on. You were about to say something."

"I'm not an underdog anymore. I got my job!"

"What job is that, Addie?"

"First, I want everybody to call me Adaira now. I think it's more elegant, and more adult, too."

"Of course, Adaira. I like that name. And what's your new job?"

"I've become an agent for Pinkerton's detective agency." Adaira threw out her arms in a wide gesture.

"My goodness. That seems so appropriate. You're always looking out for the underprivileged. And you're always searching for justice. Congratulations!"

"And she's earned her position by solving a difficult case right here in Port Gamble." Simon strode in and entered the conversation.

Ella Rose looked at him and then at Adaira. "Who are you, young man?"

"Simon Jamison, Head Agent at Pinkerton Agency in Seattle. Actually, it's a small agency right now, but it'll grow. Seattle is a booming town."

"Welcome, Simon. Let me bring you some coffee and doughnuts. You two go sit somewhere and catch your breath. I heard news that you stopped the ruckus at the mill."

Ella Rose shooed them away and brought a heaping plate of frosted doughnuts with chopped nuts sprinkled on some of them. Adaira sighed and took one.

"I don't usually indulge in these, but I'm

celebrating today." She bit a crescent out of one side and pulled the mug toward her.

"I don't like nuts," said Simon, moving his hand to a puffy doughnut glazed with white frosting.

"There are a few things we need to talk about, Agent Reagan."

"Yes?" Adaira spoke in her sweetest voice. "I have one thing I want you to do, if you please."

"What's that?"

"As I told you, my husband Sam was killed at the mill over a year ago. While I was investigating, I heard someone say that his death was no accident."

"Really?"

"Yes, so could you interrogate Hardy and Tony? You do have Tony, don't you?"

"Arrested him yesterday at the hospital."

"I can't question him, that's for sure. So, would you please do it and find out if he killed my husband?" Addie wrung her white knuckles.

"How do you know he was murdered?"

"Men at the mill said on the day of his accident, Sam caught his suspenders in the saws and was drawn in. But, that's wrong. I looked in his belongings and found his suspenders unscathed, like new. So, somebody lied. Will you investigate?"

"Of course. Now, as I was saying, there are a few things we need to talk about, Agent Reagan."

"I'm listening."

"Finally! I'll give you a letter soon saying you're officially hired. There may be a little more work around here, but after that you'll need to make your residence in Seattle."

"How will I afford that?" she said. "I don't make much now."

"You can find a boarding house, of course, but I plan to give you a raise. Now that you're off probation."

"A raise! That's wonderful." She almost hugged him, but then remembered she was the employee and he was the boss.

"Can you get your things together and move to Seattle by April?"

"I'll need to find a place to stay, but if that doesn't take long, then, yes, I can to it."

"I have a confession. The Seattle office is small. It consists of me and my secretary, Mrs. Murphy. She can help you find a boarding house."

"I'm sure I will be able to work with her," said Adaira.

"Oh, and one more thing."

"One more?"

"Yes, get a better firearm. I suggest a derringer of some kind. They're easier for a woman to handle—even a nervous woman." He looked at her with a solemn face.

"I'll try not to drop anything again, or trip over my feet." She laughed. So did he.

Adaira grabbed two more doughnuts and wrapped them in a cloth napkin. "I think my mother and father would like these. I have lots to tell them. I need to go, if you have nothing else to ask of me."

"Just one more thing," he said, and cleared his throat. "Dinner when you get settled in Seattle. I know a good restaurant."

"I never go to restaurants. Is it good?"

"Each dish is full of flavor and finely prepared."

"Sounds wonderful! I look forward to it."

Adaira put on her damp coat. "Goodbye for now." She stepped toward the door.

Simon stood. "Goodbye." He offered his hand and she took it. "Let me know if I can help in any way." She withdrew her hand before he let it go.

"Send my pay as soon as you can, please, Agent Jamison. I'm moving, but first, there's something I must do!"

❧

Addie inserted oars into the oarlocks, placed a basket on the second seat and shoved the little boat out into the bay. She grasped the shellacked handles and slid the paddles through the clear water. It wasn't far to the other shore across Gamble Bay, but Addie's hands trembled. She'd never visited a S'Klallam community.

What will I see? Will I be welcome? What can I accomplish, anyway?

Addie firmed her jaw and pulled hard on the oars. She approached the far shore rapidly. The tide was going out. She stepped out on the wet sand and rocks and grabbed the rope to pull it up farther. As she did so, an old woman walked along a shoreline path carrying a basket. Her eyes widened. She picked up her skirts and scampered away.

"Wait, please," shouted Addie. "I want to see Four Baskets." But the old woman had disappeared. Addie noticed an opening in the forest. Beyond the big tree, a group of simple houses stood together and in the middle a half dozen logs made a circle. This day, a group of natives sat on the logs, silent as gray mountains.

Addie looked for the small woman she remembered from before, Four Baskets, Eddie's wife. She finally saw her wrapped in a woven cedar bark blanket. She began a low chant, or was it a song? The Salish words were full of unusual tones and throaty noises. A few of the women took up the song. A man beat on a small drum, an animal skin stretched over a circular form. Other drums joined in and other voices, too, raising the wail. Addie stood very still and listened. It was a song of mourning and maybe a song praising the life and passing of Eddie George. She wrapped her shawl tight around her shoulders to stop the shaking. Addie bowed her head.

Please comfort Four Baskets and everyone who loved Eddie. Help her find a way to go on.

Four Baskets looked up from under the fibrous

covering and found Addie's eyes. She looked for a long moment, impassive, or was it passion held in check? Addie raised the basket she held and put it down on a prominent rock at the edge of the clearing. She smoothed the article inside.

Maybe Four Baskets can use this for her baby.

Addie nodded at Four Baskets and the Indian woman gave the smallest tip of her head in reply. Addie stepped back and returned to the rowboat.

I hope she reads the note I left or finds someone who can read it to her. I hope what I offered will be helpful. I won't need that cradle quilt any time soon.

Four Baskets deserves to be happy again.

CHAPTER 40

Caroline Murray listened carefully, her eyes big and watery. From time to time she got out her handkerchief and blew her nose. Cameron, her husband, patted her hand several times while taking in each word Adaira spoke.

"So, Mother and Father, I will need to move to Seattle in the next three weeks or so." She beamed at them.

"Addie, we're so proud—"

"Father, I'm asking everyone to call me Adaira now, but since you're family, I can make an exception. It's kind of endearing."

"All right, Addie. We'll go with you to Seattle and help you find a place and then move there." Father paused. "I hope you'll let us come visit from time to time. We love you."

"Thanks, Dad. I knew you would understand." Her mother turned to her.

"Adaira, I need to say—I'm very proud of you, too. You have chosen unusual employment, but you have succeeded. Not many young women could have accomplished what you did. I heard all about the disturbance at the mill and how you handled it."

Caroline Murray held out her arms and Adaira moved into them.

"You knew I couldn't tell you what I was really doing, don't you, Mother?"

"Yes, dear. I can't keep a secret."

"And, Mother, you do understand, I think, how losing my baby changed everything for me. I couldn't live here anymore—my whole life lost. I had nothing really to look forward to. Life looked bleak, I suppose like you felt after you were unable to have another child, Mother."

"Yes, dear, you're right," Adaira's mother sniffled and hugged her tighter.

After they separated, Adaira asked, "So, you won't oppose my move to Seattle?"

"If that's what you really want, then I won't oppose it. And I intend to visit you in Seattle." Caroline jutted her chin forward and dabbed her eyes and nose for the last time.

"Come often, Mother. It would be fun to show you around Seattle. I've heard they have all sorts of modern wonders there."

"We have lots to do." Adaira's mother stopped. "What do you want us to do?"

"Let's see if we can get a boat to Seattle tomorrow or the next day. We'll make a day of it. Mr. Jamison can make us a reservation at a boarding house for the night."

"That sounds good, Addie--Adaira," said her father. "We're with you all the way."

"Thanks for understanding, Mother and Father."

Adaira smiled at her parents and took their hands.

"I think I like the name Addie best. I'm comfortable with that. But my profession name will be Adaira." She grinned.

❧

They let go of hands and Addie went out to buy three tickets to Seattle. As she drew up to the line, she saw Chen Fu waiting, along with his wife Jiao and his son Liu.

"Hello, Chen family. What are you doing?"

"The Smith family has broken apart. Mr. Smith was arrested. So Mrs. Smith and children are packing up and will get a steamer boat soon to San Francisco."

"I'm surprised! Does Mrs. Smith know where her husband will end up?"

"She didn't say anything about it," said Mrs. Chen. She shrugged her shoulders.

"We're going to San Francisco, too. We have relatives there. We can make a new life. We heard from my uncle that my son Du has found them." Liu looked up and grinned.

"I've never seen you smile, Liu," said Adaira. "What happened to your son all these months?"

"He was put to work building a railroad line in California. Near a town called Sacramento."

"How did he find your relatives?"

"He worked and saved enough, and then walked away from the camp one night and found a stray horse to ride to San Francisco."

"Great news."

"My uncle wrote a letter the day after he got there. We only received it yesterday."

"What will you do now?"

"First we'll open a Chinese restaurant," said Mr. Chen. "Jiao is good cook," His smile broadened.

"I know that's true," said Addie. "Best of wishes to you. Good fortune." She bowed to them all.

"Maybe I will see you again sometime. I am moving to Seattle to be a detective." They congratulated her.

"Goodbye, goodbye." They all parted and waved as the distance grew between them. Addie squared her shoulders.

"Seattle, here I come. I hope you're ready for me!"

❧

"Addie, could I talk to you?" Mary Deming touched her arm.

"I was just waiting for my parents to arrive.

We're about to go explore Seattle." Addie put down her bulging carpetbag and adjusted her woolen shawl.

"You're leaving Port Gamble?"

"Not quite yet, but yes, in a few weeks." Mary fidgeted with her hands, smoothing her shawl. "I've enjoyed our talks recently," said Addie.

"So have I. You've helped me to think things through about my husband."

"How is he doing, Mary?"

"That's what I came to tell you. He just turned himself into the hospital. He's asked Dr. Spencer to restrain him, so he doesn't take that evil liquid, chloroform."

"So, that's what was bothering him. Chloroform?"

"Yes."

"I'm amazed. I thought that was only used for surgery."

"It should be. John came in contact with it when he was stitching people up after some mill accidents. Says it has an enticing aroma."

"But it's dangerous to sniff it. It puts you to sleep."

"Yes, that's the tricky part. It must be used very carefully."

"Is that what happened to him after the sermon last week?"

"Yes, I told everyone it was a heart ailment, but it was too much chloroform." Mary gulped. "He almost died. And, of course, the incident when he fainted while taking the children to school."

"I'm so sorry."

"Those brushes with death caused John to think about what he was doing. He's tied to this medicine and can't get free. He says he has to have it."

"What?"

"He wants to be free, but he doesn't have the power. So he asked Dr. Spencer for help. Dr. Spencer has found a place that takes people with his problem. A sober house, it's called. There's a new one in Port Townsend, I've heard."

"For people who are drunkards?"

"Or addicted to certain medicines."

"Where are you going? Will you come back?"

"It all depends on John. He's taken a leave of absence. Please don't tell anyone the real reason."

"I won't, I promise, Mary."

"We're leaving tomorrow. I just have to pack our clothes and prepare the children."

"You're going, too?"

"I can't stay with him in the hospital, but I can visit him when he progresses to a certain point."

"I truly hope it works. He's a good man, Mary. I'll pray for his recovery."

"Thank you, Addie. You're a true friend."

"I'm moving to Seattle soon, but I'll leave my address with my parents. If you come back, look me up. I'm going to be a detective for Pinkerton's Agency."

"How professional you'll be!"

"Best wishes, Mary." Addie embraced her friend.

"I'll see you in six months." Mary hugged her and then turned and left.

Just then, Caroline and Cameron Murray, Addie's parents, joined her at the dock.

"Was that Pastor Deming's wife you were talking to?"

"Mary? Yes. She said goodbye."

"We're ready to go, and I see the steamship rounding the bend over there." Mr. Murray pulled out his pocket watch. "Right on time."

"Well, we're off to Seattle for sure, now. Let's enjoy the trip. I hear it's great."

"Right you are."

"It's so exciting," said Caroline Murray. "My first trip to the big city."

"Seattle, here we come," they all said together. Then Addie laughed.

"Let's go!"

A Note from
the Author

I grew up in Seattle, boarding the ferry system often to explore the Northwest. My sister and I rode the rattling monsters with our mother across Puget Sound to Suquamish and our friends' summer place. I leaned over the railing to watch for jellyfish in the indigo waters. Lopez Island held another family's cabin, quirky with a menagerie of carved animal sculptures. Most of all, I remember how Uncle Ed and Aunt Ruth invited us every summer to ride the Edmonds-Kingston ferry to their place on Gamble Bay. All the kids and cousins rode in the back of the truck on little wooden stools. We spent the day swimming and turning blue in the cold saltwater and then flopping up onto the float to get some sun. We had to wear flip-flops all the time to avoid scraping toes on the barnacled rocks of the beach. Later on, we roasted hot dogs and marshmallows and ate watermelon. Of course, we had a seed-spitting contest.

Their summer place was close to Port Gamble, but I don't remember ever visiting the historic town with them. Many years later I've come to appreciate this premier logging town. Now, I live near enough to drive by it about once a week.

Port Gamble began in 1853, when Andrew J. Pope and Frederic Talbot sailed into Gamble Bay and declared it the perfect place to start a lumber mill. They both came from Maine and recruited some of their first workers from East Machias, their hometown. The Pope & Talbot headquarters had been established in San Francisco, to supply lumber for the California Gold Rush.

The mill and town survived and thrived for almost one hundred and fifty years. They weathered the Civil War, economic panics at the end of the nineteenth century, the Alaska Gold Rush that drained the worker pool, two world wars, and the need to replace old machines with modern and efficient equipment. Members of the family still credit this longevity to good New England values, such as debt aversion and the integrity of the management.

Originally, the pace of life was monotonous and grueling in the mill community. In 1889, the time in which this novel is set, shifts lasted eleven and a half hours, the food was plain but filling, and each worker received their pay in fifty-cent pieces. Accidents were frequent. For every man who quit in exhaustion, another was willing and ready to assume the risks and the burdensome toil. Sawdust and the whine of saws filled the air constantly.

The management tried to keep the men and families happy by arranging an abundance of activities. Socials of all kinds occupied them. A community hall was built, and a school established to attract families. Other amenities included a barbershop, bowling alley and dance hall. Holidays included only Christmas, Thanksgiving and Independence Day. Maple trees lined the streets and picket fences kept the company pigs and horses from trampling the yards.

Port Gamble was known for its excellent baseball team. They challenged teams from other local sawmills and communities around the Kitsap Peninsula. The management discouraged gambling and drinking at Port Gamble, but naturally there were places off-site where these enticements could be found. They didn't dare prohibit alcohol, though.

The Port Gamble house of worship, founded in 1870, began as a Congregational church, but it later became Episcopalian. There really was a Pastor John Damon at Port Gamble. I changed the name to show his story here is fictional. A cryptic note under his picture in the museum says he was called the "marrying preacher" and that he used chloroform to help him deliver his sermons. Another historical character I included in *Trouble at Port Gamble* is Edwin Ames, a good and apparently honest manager who arrived in 1888 and promptly built a large mansion (now called Walker-Ames House) that faced the bay rather than the street it occupied. Ames invited people who docked at the pier to dinner in his house. His hospitality led to increased sales. He made many improvements in mill operations. His part in the plot here is also fictional.

A third historical character is Frank Hall, based on the real-life Frank Finkel (or Finkle) that claimed to be the lone white survivor of the Battle of Little Bighorn. He stated his horse bolted through Indian battle lines and kept going. No Sioux tracked him down. His horse died of over-exertion. Finkel collapsed from two wounds at a cabin in the woods. The man there took him in and let him recover over the next six months. It was only recently proved that what he said was true. Historians compared his signature on his will to his signature on his enlistment papers. By the way, he settled in Dayton, Washington, and became quite successful in farming. He died in 1930.

The S'Klallam, a Salish-speaking people, lived at the body of water that was later named Gamble Bay by white settlers. The S'Klallam were called the Nux Sklai Yem, Strong People. The S'Klallam called the place Teekalet, "brightness of the noon day sun." When white people came on steamships in 1853, they bargained with the native peoples to get them to move across the bay to Point Julia. They helped build houses there, also.

S'Klallam men worked in the sawmill. They canoed over from Point Julia, just across Gamble Bay. Chinese people worked in both mill jobs and as cooks and servers in the hotel and mess hall. They always lived separately from the other workers.

Pope & Talbot underwent many changes between 1940 and 1980. They altered their business strategy from resources to developing new products in wood, pulp and absorbent paper. They re-tooled the machinery, away from large diameter, old-growth timber to small logs. They planted and managed tree farms, developed pulp for newsprint and napkins and made hardboard and plywood products.

Pope & Talbot had invested heavily in developing Port Ludlow. Houses were built and a great inn was completed on the site of the former Port Ludlow mill, at a cost of over five million dollars. House sales stalled when a large septic system was called for. Always, they had to think of ways to capitalize and reduce debt.

Although Pope & Talbot survived when many other competitors failed, its future was in doubt by the early 1980s. To discourage a corporate takeover bid, the management decided to offer shares on the Pacific Stock Exchange. Before that, all capital had come from internally generated funds. In December 1985, Pope & Talbot stockholders approved a plan to create a limited partnership called Pope Resources, Inc., as a manufacturing entity. The assets were divided between the two entities, with Pope Resources receiving all the Washington timber—76,000 acres—and Port Gamble mill site and town.

The new company received Port Ludlow and 4,400 acres of undeveloped land in Oregon and Washington, as well. Pope & Talbot retained all manufacturing centers, logging rights in British Columbia and the Black Hills, and the remaining 40,000 acres of the Penn Tract. It leased Port Gamble to keep the mill running and took over management of the town site. About that time, Port Gamble was designated an historic site.

Many more events transpired in its history, but Port Gamble's mill finally closed on November 30, 1995, with only twenty remaining employees. The mill was no longer profitable, so Pope & Talbot had to cease operations and sell off the equipment. The mill at Port Gamble was the longest operating U.S. sawmill (142 years). *Pope Resources: Rooted in the Past, Growing for the Future,* by Harry Stein, tells the story well.

I've learned so much about Port Gamble's history and have come to appreciate the rugged men and women who lived, worked and died there.

I hope you enjoyed your trip back into the Washington Territory of 1889. Addie will experience other adventures as she embraces her new job and new life.

Read the further exploits of Addie in *Feeling the Heat in Seattle*, coming soon.

Beryl Carpenter
December 2019

Printed in the United States
By Bookmasters